AF440688

THE MACKIN COVER

THE MACKIN COVER

A novel of suspense by
DIANE K. SHAH

DODD, MEAD & COMPANY
New York

Library of Congress Cataloging in Publication Data

Shah, Diane K
  The Mackin Cover.
  I. Title.
PZ4.S52663Mac [PS3569.H314] 813'.5'4 77–22710
ISBN 0–396–07511–8

FOR BRUCE, who always understood, and
with special thanks to RICHARD HUGHES

Chapter 1

Alexander Mackin didn't look at all like a man about to die.

Rather, as he stood scowling into his medicine cabinet, he looked the picture of blooming health. There was his size—six-feet-three, the record books said—and 210 pounds, but indecently, not an ounce of fat on him, at least none that could be detected through the blue knit shirt and skin-tight jeans. No sign of death pallor either, just a nice even tan. Then the cabinet door banged shut, and briefly, before he turned to me, I caught his reflection in the mirror.

It was the eyes you noticed first, large and green with those interesting black flecks. Then, maybe, the tiny scar over the pale right eyebrow. Or the sun-bleached hair and, just a tad darker in shade, the full mustache that nicely offset the prominent nose and wide mouth. It wasn't a classically handsome face, but sexy all the same. No, not sexy. Just intensely male, like all the rest of him . . . slightly larger than life.

He was also paranoid.

Only hours earlier, Alexander Mackin had been directing his team to another American Football Conference title—a decisive 28 to 7 win over Pittsburgh. Yet instead of getting a blow-by-blow account of the game, I was stuck on his tub getting a clinical analysis of all his medicines. It was a nice collection. But not exactly what I'd come 3,000 miles for. And now it was nearly midnight.

"That," he said with complaint in his voice, "doesn't even

include all the crap they shoot into you before a game."

I cut into his litany of what was wrong. "You mean," I said vaguely, "you might retire . . . because you don't like taking your medicine?"

Mackin looked at me impatiently. "You just don't understand."

"Understand what?"

"That I'm going to die. Probably soon."

"Oh."

I glanced quickly away so as not to laugh and noticed *The Merck Manual of Diagnosis and Therapy* lying open on the toilet. It was exactly the size of a prayer book. Two inches thick and worn as a priest's.

Mackin nudged a hip onto the shocking yellow sink and began massaging his right knee. I couldn't help but smile. I had yet to meet an athlete who didn't constantly fiddle with some part of his sacred anatomy.

"Okay," I said, "so you've got a bad knee. You also," I reminded him, "threw for three touchdowns this afternoon. If you ask me, you're more deadly than deathly."

Mackin cocked his head sideways and gave me the full benefit of his dazzling green eyes. "Listen," he said urgently, "when you're thirty years old and you've had the kind of life no man deserves, then you have to wonder. When do you pay up?"

I looked at the brandy snifter and the bottle of Courvoisier perched on the back of his tub. "I wouldn't know," I told him. "I haven't had that kind of life."

"But it makes sense, doesn't it? What else can there be?"

He spoke with conviction. I took notes with skepticism. After all, a guy doesn't become a national celebrity just because he throws a good pass. He's got to be good press, too. And this one was. So maybe he was merely trying another gimmick. An athlete dying young who could only be saved by a healthy, new contract.

2

"Maybe," I said, shifting on the tub, "you've been reading too much Housman." I had noticed a book of his poems in Mackin's living room. But I wondered if he had read them. Or any of the impressive titles all lined up out there on his custom-built shelves.

Mackin shrugged. He sighed. He offered me what I gathered was supposed to be the sheepish grin of a man who had just uttered a secret confidence—then regretted it. I had to hand it to him. He had done a masterful job of setting me up for this one. All night long he had been altering his moods, changing his stories, taking control of *my* interview the way he took control of his offense. And I still didn't know if this was the finale—or if there were more. I had badly underrated him. Clearly he was not a typical dumb jock.

Mackin turned and began inspecting his face in the mirror, rubbing his jaw for signs of stubble. Suddenly he burst out laughing.

"It's funny?"

"No," he replied, swiveling round. "But it just occurred to me that I've never been interviewed in a john, for crissake." He grinned broadly. "Which, uh, reminds me. You still haven't seen my bedroom."

I got up from the tub. Stood there facing him, meeting those ingenuous green eyes, which as always, revealed nothing. But it was more than the eyes, it was something else. Call it presence. Or maybe it was that withheld quality of his, he gave very little and made you want more. I noticed again how big he was —small beside other players, but not in this room—and how well he held himself, and how the muscles bulged in his fore-arms and flowed so smoothly down to the tanned and powerful wrists.

And then it struck me that it was too quiet and that I had been staring at him and maybe thinking things I shouldn't have. I became suddenly conscious of how ridiculous I must have looked standing there clutching my notebook. I needed to say something, but couldn't think what, and then, absurdly, the doorbell chimed.

Mackin's eyes widened, slid from me to his watch. "Now who . . . ?"

"The undertaker?" I suggested.

He didn't think that was funny, he said, as he hurried to answer the door.

As it turned out, it wasn't.

Shortly before midnight, Alexander Mackin said he was afraid he was going to die. Some time after midnight on Monday, December 31, Alexander Mackin disappeared.

As usual, his timing was perfect.

**Chapter 2**

"You call this journalism?" Maxwell fumed. "I call it _fiction._"

Exasperatedly, my editor turned the last sheet of copy paper face down on top of the others and began drumming his fingers on the glass-topped desk. I watched the smudges form, along with the frown, and waited for the rest of it.

"And you know how I feel about the I," he said crossly.

That, I did. James R. Maxwell, managing editor of _Monday_ magazine, strongly disapproved of writers using the first person singular, and then there was the bathroom, right up there in the lead. Under the circumstances, I had hoped to get away with it. But I should have known better with a man who still advocated Webster's Second Edition, and that only because the First Edition had inexplicably gone out of print. Webster's Third was grounds for dismissal.

He tapped my story. "Maybe you can get away with your snide sarcasm when you're writing for the back of the book," he said shortly, "but not," he tapped my story again, "when you're writing for my _cover._"

"He isn't retiring," I said in mild defense.

Maxwell reached for his red grease pencil, always a bad omen. As usual, he was wearing a white shirt and narrow striped tie. I doubted that he had changed his appearance one iota since 1959, the date engraved on the Harvard Business School diploma, framed and stationed on the window sill be-

_5_

hind him. Still frowning, he began sifting through the pages anew, as if willing them to metamorphose into language he liked.

"I mean what is this nonsense?" he demanded." 'Mackin disappeared. As usual his timing was perfect'?"

"Perhaps it was a bit frivolous," I conceded. "It's just that with Mackin you're never quite sure when you can trust him."

"To disappear?"

"It's worth investigating."

"Lindsie," he growled, "I sent you to find out if the man is retiring from football, as he claims, and if so, why. And you come back three days later with this absurd nonsense about a disappearance. Where's your authority?" He began marking my copy with bold, slashing strokes.

I said, "When I woke up Monday morning he was gone. Nobody seems to know just where he is."

Maxwell looked up. "That's a good start," he shot back. "For a novel. Try getting some facts next time."

"I'll get the facts," I pleaded.

Maxwell shook his head and kept hacking away. "You've never let us down before," he said accusingly.

My prose was bleeding to death under the merciless jabbing of his hungry red pencil. I looked away. Outside the window, snowflakes were fluttering drearily into the gray Boston Harbor. I shivered inwardly. It was a cold office to begin with, more a reflection of personality than thermostat. At right angles to the panoramic window were built-in bookshelves, each book perfectly aligned, just like the framed covers of a dozen magazines that hung on the wall behind me. And then there were the visitor's chairs, planted an annoying three feet from the enormous desk to give Maxwell the psychological advantage. Which, of course, he held anyway.

I shifted in one of them and glanced at the chessboard, set

at one corner of the immaculate desk. It had been a gift from a grand master we had once done a cover on. Nobody seemed to know if Maxwell actually played, but the office joke was that the chessmen represented the staff.

"That's what you get," I said flippantly, "for sending a pawn to capture a knight."

An eyebrow arched menacingly. "I just don't understand your attitude, Lindsie. There isn't a reporter here who wouldn't give his eye teeth to do a football story. And here you're sent to interview the NFL's top quarterback. You of all people . . ." He let the sentence drift.

"I'll take another shot at it," I promised.

Maxwell gathered the pages together and started to slide them across the desk. Then halted abruptly. "Just a moment," he said. "I didn't see anything in here about his legs."

"I don't think it's his legs," I answered. "I don't think it's anything at all."

"No," said Maxwell emphatically. "Not according to what I heard. You should have checked it out."

I felt my anger rising. One of the annoying things about Maxwell is that he plays games. He will hear something, then will mention it—that is, part of it—to a reporter. Knowing the whole story himself, he'll make the reporter do all the leg work. And sometimes, just as a test, he'll throw out a tidbit that won't wash at all. I wasn't sure if what Maxwell had was solid, but I doubted it.

"Look," I tried again, "why would he retire? He's at the height of his career. Besides, he's retired before. Every time his contract comes up. He's only playing games."

Maxwell leaned forward and reached for his pipe. "Did it ever occur to you," he said mildly, "that his games just might be intended to make you think he's *not* retiring?"

I thought that over for a moment. But it didn't particularly turn me on. "All right," I said. "I'll do some more checking. In the meantime, er, about his disappearance . . ."

Maxwell cut me off with an impatient wave of his pipe. "If Alex Mackin's disappeared," he said calmly, "we'll know soon enough. He's due to arrive in New Orleans on Thursday. And your story," he reminded me, "is due on Friday."

Already his gaze had shifted to the chessboard, his way of signaling dismissal. I picked up the remains of my story and walked out the door.

I returned to my office on the 34th floor, down six stories and a long drop in status from Maxwell's penthouse. Actually, office was a rather flashy name for my ten by twelve cubicle, one of sixty identical rooms assigned senior, associate, and contributing editors. Like the others, mine was furnished with a coat rack, a bookcase, a blue metal filing cabinet, and two blue metal desks. One of the desks had a pair of feet on it. My researcher put down his magazine and glanced up.

"Welcome back from heaven," said Tom Eastwick.

"Heaven?" I said. "I thought you were into nirvana these days."

He grinned. "So? How was Mackin?"

I sat down at my desk. "I suppose you expected me to bring you an autograph?"

"Oh, come on, Lindsie. He's a neat guy."

"Maybe in person," I said. "But he doesn't translate well onto paper. Maxwell didn't like my story."

Tom immediately perked up. "Good," he declared. "Maybe next time they'll send *me.*"

Tom Eastwick was a recent Princeton graduate who held ill-concealed hopes of one day ascending to the top of the masthead. For the past six months, he had been trying to ascend over me.

"I'll carry your bags to the airport," I said. "Just get Maxwell to take me off football."

Tom laughed and swiveled round to answer his phone. I picked up my ravaged story and dropped it into the wastebasket. Then I sat stewing for not having stood up to Maxwell. I had known, of course, even before I set foot on his priceless Chinese rug, what his reaction would be. That Mackin knew the men. That I had no hard evidence anything had happened to him. That nobody seemed concerned when he abruptly left home.

Nobody, except me, Lindsie Hollis, one of 30 writers with an associate editor's title on the door and not a shred of carpet on the floor. Nor much prospect of getting one. John Pinckney Blodgett, *Monday's* publisher, was an elderly, gracious, tightwad, who had established the magazine in Boston because the real estate was cheaper than New York's. No matter that the cost of our Government Center offices had gone through the roof. As long as Harvard remained a stone's throw away, we would be stationed in Boston and staffed with Hasty Pudding types, except for the few interlopers hired to keep the federal government off Blodgett's back.

I was one of them.

I sighed and slid a fresh sheet of copy paper into my typewriter, lit a cigarette and glanced restlessly around my office. Tom's bicycle wheel leaned against the window, his plants covered the sill. If he didn't take over my job, he soon would take over my office.

I typed the words, "Memo to Maxwell," and got annoyed all over again. I hadn't wanted the assignment in the first place. I never did when it came to football. Unfortunately, my being the daughter of a head coach appealed to Maxwell's sense of orderliness. No matter that Dad's team was one of the losingest in the NFL. Whenever there was more than a routine football story to be done, I was Maxwell's choice. Or pawn. Or in this case . . . maybe Mackin's.

"From Hollis," I added to the page, and wondered again about Alex Mackin, the superstud football player who was either up to his gorgeous neck in trouble, or yukking it up beside some mountain stream at the con he had pulled on me. The freak accident of being born with an arm both sure and strong had allowed him to do anything he wanted to on the field. And from what I gathered, he seemed to carry the same attitude off it. Good looks, charm, and an uncanny sense of knowing what the press wanted to hear, had all combined to make Mackin more than just a football star. He was also hero to millions who didn't know a draw play from a double play—and didn't care.

I reached for the thick file sitting on my "Out" basket and began flipping idly through the memos, the clips, the yellowed wire service stories. It was all there. Mackin winning the Heisman Trophy at USC. Mackin the first-round draft pick of the last-place San Diego Chargers. That first season the team turned in a winning record. The second season it took a division title. The third season, the Super Bowl. His contract holdouts. His relentlessly chronicled social life. All of it neatly stacked in my worn manilla folder like an advertising man's wishful thinking. For had Mackin been dreamed up by Madison Avenue, he could not have been more perfectly packaged as Mr. Superstud Jock. He even had a book, *The Quintessential Quarterback,* in which he had said, among other things, that all females could be divided into four categories—broads, birds, chics, and women—I forget the distinctions.

And yet. He was not so easily typecast.

For if Mackin made sure that every step of his whereabouts was faithfully reported during the season, from January to mid-July he inexplicably vanished from print—and from sight.

Unlike other athletes, he lent his name to no charitable cause, held no summer football camps for teenaged boys, was conspicuously absent from TV talk shows. And while he was outrageous in his salary demands, he routinely turned down millions of dollars in endorsements, allowing his name to be used only in connection with one shaving cream.

All this I had learned from my research, and still it hadn't prepared me. Nothing I had read about the man in our clip file on Friday seemed to fit the man I had met in San Diego on Sunday.

He was an enigma then. And he was an enigma now.

I stubbed out my cigarette and typed, "Re Mackin."

Chapter 3

It had been a cool Sunday evening in San Diego.

Even the lingering rays of sunshine no longer carried much warmth. Behind the wrought-iron gate, the long shadows of the palm trees fell across the sweep of lawn and spilled onto the circular drive. A wedge of sun still peeked over the red-tiled roof but soon it would be gone and I could imagine how the place would look when it was all lighted up. Like a minor Mexican palace. I stuffed my notebook into my purse, locked my little red Toyota, and wandered across the street.

The gravel made a nice crunching noise as I walked up the drive. A man in blue jeans was polishing a Mercedes. I stepped around him and up to the front door.

A sign said, "All Visitors, Please Ring." I studied the two rows of buttons and was just about to push the one marked "Mackin," when the door flew open and a small boy scurried out. I caught the brass doorknob and slipped inside only to find myself in a wide, open-ended passageway laid with Spanish tile.

I followed it through to the back of the building and out to a small oval swimming pool. Beyond it lay landscaped terraces with all manner of bougainvillae, eucalyptus, capa de oro, and azalea. Far below, the spray of the Pacific Ocean caught the last rays of sunshine and glistened like handfuls of cut diamonds. Which, at this address, they probably were.

The building overlooking all this was two stories high with two wings reaching out toward the ocean. A wrought-iron staircase led me to the second floor, and after taking a right turn I found Mackin's apartment, last of the lot. Number 20, it said in brass script lettering. I rang the bell, rang it twice, and wandered back to the stairs. Below me, the pool lay empty, the deck chairs folded and neatly stacked, the table umbrellas tied down. Sounds and dinner smells wafted out the windows, and the occasional tenant hurrying by barely flicked me an indifferent glance as I sat on the steps like a forlorn child who had forgotten the house key.

An hour later, in the pitch darkness, I began to wonder if Mackin had forgotten me.

On the phone the night before, he had grudgingly consented to see me after the game—providing the Chargers won it. Naturally I had agreed, because I had told him we were doing an advance story on the Super Bowl. I was afraid if I had told him flat out what I wanted he would have—flat out—turned me down. For some unknown reason Alexander Mackin was refusing to talk about his latest "retirement." He had not even gone about announcing it in the usual way.

What he had done, more or less, was whisper it.

According to the story I heard, Mackin had been heading out the door after practice one afternoon when he stopped to chat with Wade Hampton, the Chargers' second-string quarterback. He had said something to the effect, "Cheer up, old buddy. It'll be your team next year. Uncle Alex won't be around."

A local reporter just happened to be coming out of Coach Charlie Sims' office at that very moment and overheard what Mackin said. He printed it. The wire services picked it up. The networks carried it. And Mackin was besieged. Yet while he refused to deny it, he also refused to elaborate on it.

This was somewhat out of character. Typical Mackin retirements—there had already been two—took on the bathos of a soap opera. But then, when you've thrown forty-one touchdown passes in a single season, set more passing records than any other quarterback, and are personally credited with transforming a failing franchise into one of football's most fearsome teams—you can get away with anything.

Eight forty-five. At the moment he was getting away with murder. I stamped out my cigarette and found myself rubbing my hands together. It had grown quite chill and the sound of the waves beating on shore only made it feel colder. But then, I was an old hand at waiting on damp doorsteps for football men. My father had never been home after school. He'd be down at the practice field with my older brothers, working them out like regular members of the team. His hope was that they'd follow him into the business. They hadn't. And he didn't seem particularly consoled that I had. I was hungry.

Time passed.

Had it been anyone else, I would have left. But when Alex Mackin says he's going to retire—even if it's his third threat— you've got to check it out just in case he actually means it. And through some labyrinthian deduction, trifling chess move or secret source, Maxwell seemed sure that he did.

Nine-fifty.

I lit another cigarette and dropped the match between the stairs onto the growing pile of butts below. And then I spotted him, long before he noticed me huddled on the darkened stairs. He was wearing jeans, a blue knit shirt, and some kind of crazy-colored running shoes. A navy nylon jacket was slung over one shoulder. I put out my cigarette just as the blond, tousled head peeked around the railing.

"Alex?"

His head jerked up in surprise. "Yes?"

"I'm Lindsie Hollis . . ."

"So?"

The camera freezes one facial expression through which the

entire personality is shaped. So that in person, Mackin looked less narrowly defined, more bland. "So you won."

He gave me a sharp unfriendly glance. "I know I won. So what?"

"So I guess you forgot."

"Oh, Christ," said Mackin frowning. "Don't tell me I promised you tickets to the Super Bowl?"

There wasn't much light coming down from the upper balcony and I wasn't sure from his tone if he were serious. "No," I said, standing up. "But you did promise me an interview." He just looked at me. "*Monday* magazine?" I said helpfully.

Mackin grimaced. "Yeah, well, it's still only Sunday." He started up the stairs past me. I grabbed his elbow as he tried to shoulder by. A good seven inches and ninety pounds he had on me. I hung on anyway.

"Look," I said, positioning the corners of my mouth upwards a fraction, "it'll only take an hour." His elbow felt like a small boulder.

Mackin grinned back, though not in a particularly nice way. "It's for a cover story," I added. I forced another smile, but it didn't sit too well, either on my face or with Mackin. He yanked his elbow free.

"Oh, sure," he said, "a cover story. You and all those lady reporters with their cover stories." With that, he went up a step, turned, and struck a rather ludicrous pose. "Beith there no cover so desired by a fair lady," he recited, "than the cover of a warm-blooded man." He smirked and marched up the stairs.

"Or maybe," I called after him, " 'These are the times that try men's souls'?"

"Right," said Mackin from the landing. "So why don't you try someone else's soul? Mine's tired." Again he started to move away.

I almost let him go. For I was irked at being put in the

position of having to beg. Or plead. Or worse, fawn. One had to at times. And I hated it. But it suddenly struck me Mackin was behaving all wrong. Mackin, who stood in the dressing room answering every last question. Mackin, who went out of his way to accommodate any reporter's whim for a story. A renowned athlete who allowed his phone number to be given out to reporters . . .

Even if he had forgotten me, even if it were late, Alexander Mackin never turned a reporter away . . . not ever. Suddenly, I was interested.

"You're right," I said quickly. "It *is* kind of late. If you could just let me use your telephone . . ."

Mackin stopped, turned, walked back a couple of steps, and peered down at me. Then he smiled. A nice boyish grin showing all those nice white teeth.

"And then maybe," he said mockingly, "just a small cup of coffee? And while you're drinking it, just one or two teeny little questions?"

He had come down a step and was leaning forward with his hands grasping the railings. In the half-light he looked almost demonic.

I hesitated. "Er . . . do you have any cream?"

Chapter 4

Mackin's apartment was neither bachelor-pad cool nor single-man sloppy. It wasn't overfurnished, it wasn't too bare. It had all the comforts of home and yet, it wasn't a comfortable home. What it was exactly . . . I couldn't say.

"It's over there," he said pointing.

I yanked my attention from the barreling elephants, not fifteen feet in front of me, and followed his fingertip to a jungle of leafy, unkempt plants scattered about the bare floor off to the right. Begun undoubtedly as some decorator's idea of art, it had failed miserably under Mackin's clumsy plant care. Through the sad, droopy leaves loomed a bored-looking hippopotamus. The large leather kind you can pick up at Abercrombie's for a small green fortune.

"What is?"

"The phone. But then, you didn't really want to use it, did you?" He shrugged. "Well, make yourself at home while I find some coffee. You did want coffee?"

"If it's not too much trouble."

As he vanished through a doorway straight ahead, I took a closer look at the quarterback's household. Fully one-third of the spacious living room was given over to the plants, including a couple of dehydrated palms, which clawed at the sliding glass doors leading onto a balcony. That was stage right. In the center of the room, upon a thick cream carpet, stood a brown velvet couch, a glass coffee table, and two armchairs. Stage left,

17

squatting lonesomely on a dark brown rug sat a small dining table supporting a film projector; and up against the far wall, a built-in bar. Bamboo shades lined the windows to the left of the bar; teakwood bookshelves the wall to the right. Scattered among the many books were pieces of African sculpture. Not plasticine copies either. The real thing. A stereo, too, and a color TV. All very tasteful—and yet. Somehow all wrong. I couldn't quite put my finger on it.

A cabinet door slammed shut and my gaze returned to the elephants, hung on the wall between two doorways. Through one of those doorways came Mackin, carrying a glass of milk in one hand and a jar of instant coffee in the other. He thrust the jar under my nose. "What do you think?"

I looked at the grayish powder. "I think," I said, "that I don't want the coffee either."

"Milk then? Or beer?"

"No, thank you."

He set the jar on the coffee table, sat down on the couch, nudged off his shoes, and threw his legs up onto the table, barely missing an elephant tusk. "You might as well sit down," he said grudgingly.

I sat on one of the leather arm chairs and decided maybe it was the lighting. There were no lamps, just inset lights, which cast eerie shadows on the dark, leafy jungle. And had the effect of drawing you right back to Mackin.

"Let's get it over with," he said forbiddingly.

I dug into my shoulder bag for pen and notebook while his catlike green eyes watched me over the rim of his milk glass. He belched, put down the glass, and began stroking his mustache. There was something sensuous about the way he did it; and something defiant.

"I suppose you're a sports reporter?"

"Sort of."

"And you really understand football?"

"Well . . ."

"What don't you understand?"

"The players," I said.

"That's funny," he said. "Because I don't understand reporters. I mean what kind of charge do you get poking into people's
lives?"

"I think," I said, "the word you are looking for is probing."

Mackin shrugged. "So probe. But could you be kind of gentle? I bruise easy."

He was trying to put me on the defensive, a place I didn't
want to be. Slowly, I lit a cigarette and asked, "Where did you
get the elephant tusk?"

He grinned. "From an elephant."

"For an autograph?"

Mackin ignored my sarcasm. "I spent some time in Kenya,"
he said. "On one of those photographic safaris. We came across
a dead elephant and I cut off the tusk."

"You take pictures?" The sudden image of such a large man
squinting through a tiny viewfinder struck me as ludicrous.

Mackin twisted around. "See those elephants? I had an artist
screen print that from one of my photographs. Those pictures
over the bar, they're mine, too."

"Is there anything else you do?"

He grinned.

"Okay, so how are your legs?"

"Not as nice as your's." He yawned. I said nothing.

Having got no reaction from me, he stretched his arms over
his head and consulted his watch. "Sorry, got to run," he said
without apology. "Call me tomorrow if you need anything else,
okay?"

"Fine." I stood up. Looked at him, sprawled lazily on the
couch, watching me expressionlessly, except for the eyes. They

held amusement. I didn't speak, nor did he. And from somewhere in the jungle came the faint ticking of a clock. Seconds
passed. And still I did not speak. He had dumped the ball
squarely in my court and I wasn't going to send it back.

"Then again," he said slowly, "this evening could end another away."

"No," I said quietly. "That isn't why I came."

"Why did you come?"

"You know why."

"You people," he said bitterly. "Did *Monday* really think I'd
talk just because they sent a pretty reporter?"

"Does Alex Mackin really think any body believes he's actually going to retire?"

"You do. Or you wouldn't be here."

"No," I said. "I don't believe it at all. You're just playing
games. But how long do you think you can go on kidding
people? People who make so much less than you. How long do
you think they'll care?"

"As long as people like you keep coming around."

He was right about that, I thought, as I stuffed my notebook
into my purse. "Thanks, Alex."

I started for the door. But only because I knew he wouldn't
let me go. If he hadn't wanted to tell me something, he wouldn't
have let me come in.

"I'd see you out," came the voice from the couch, "but I have
a bad knee. Sorry."

Halfway to the door, I paused.

"It's a funny thing," he went on. "The knee. You can play
with a dislocated shoulder, a broken arm, cracked ribs. But the
knee—you can't fool around with a knee."

I turned back to him. He was idly pulling on his mustache,
but watching me all the same, waiting to see if I'd play his game.

There was a long silence. I understood what he was doing,

but not why. I needed time. I said, "May I look at your sculpture?"

He shrugged and I walked over to the bookshelves. I knew nothing about African art, but Maxwell would want the book titles. It was an eclectic assortment from what I could glimpse. College texts on nineteenth century English literature, volumes on medicine, popular novels, an impressive collection of journals on marine biology of all things, several books on Africa including Robert Ardrey's *African Genesis,* a biography of General MacArthur, something called *Ordering in French,* two gourmet cookbooks, *Semi-Tough,* and everything Hemingway ever wrote.

I moved slowly around to the bar and studied the photographs hanging behind it. One picture showed a half-submerged hippopotamus against an artistically out-of-focus foreground. There was a nice shot of an elephant snatching some leaves; another of a man in a safari suit. And absolutely none of it jibed.

As I sat down, Mackin was still watching me with amused eyes, refusing to give anything away. "What do you think of Ardrey?" I asked.

He frowned. "Ardrey? What team's he with?"

"The Australopithecines?"

Mackin nodded. "Right. The A's. Not much on size but good killer instincts."

He said it earnestly, except his voice couldn't quite hide the mockery . . . An apartment filled with books, art, and photographs of Africa . . . And that's when it hit me. It wasn't the lighting. It wasn't anything that was there. But instead of seeing it for what it was, I had been searching the empty places for what should have been. The trophies, the pictures in uniform, a game ball or two, the proud mementos displayed by all athletes. Except this one. This one left his football at the stadium to come home to a strange, lonely apartment so at odds with his public persona. Someone, I thought wryly, was kidding someone, but I wasn't sure whom.

"About your knee . . ."

"What about it?"

"I'm sorry, but you'll have to explain—"

"It's after eleven," Mackin said sharply.

"I'm sorry. I won't be much longer."

He sighed heavily. "All right, look. I got may be five good years left, 'cause no matter how much tape I use or pills I take, my legs are gonna fall apart. And you can write that down."

I pulled out my notebook and jotted that down.

"You can play with pain in the knee but that's not the point." Whatever his point, he came over and sat on the edge of the coffee table to make it.

"The point," he said, "is what you're doing to your legs. Hell, I could practically hear the cartilage rattling around today. After a while, you lose enough cartilage and that's it. And I'll be damned if I'm gonna spend the rest of my life a cripple for a few good years. I'm not going to end up like Namath. Can you understand *that?*"

"Yes."

"And there was another guy, too. Sammy Hines, played a few years back. Did he ever mess up his knees! Some days the poor bastard can't even get out of bed."

"I understand," I said.

"Fine. Is there anything else?"

He was sitting only a foot away and I could detect a hint of Aramis. Appreciatively, I sniffed again and said, "Well . . . yes. What I don't understand is why you're so concerned about becoming crippled."

"Jesus," he exploded. "Do I have to go through it again?"

"Not at all," I said patiently. "Just the truth this time."

I could see a flash of meanness in his eyes and I could imagine how the opposition felt when they saw it, too. For one frightening moment he seemed capable of anything.

I said quickly, "That torn cartilage you got at the end of last season was one of the few leg injuries you've had. There have been ankle sprains and pulled hamstrings. And bruised ribs and that shoulder separation your second year. Outside of that, you've been amazingly healthy—or lucky. And your bad right knee is the result of a light sprain you suffered in practice last week. The torn cartilage has healed." I paused. "Alex, who are you trying to kid?"

The look of fury had dissipated into one of uncertainty. Abruptly he stood up. "Come here, Lucy. I want to show you something."

"Only it's Lindsie," I said. "Lindsie Hollis." I smiled. "At least you could get my name right."

Chapter 5

I followed his stiff back through the second doorway abutting the elephants, down a hall, and into a bathroom. Crossly, he flung open the medicine cabinet and jabbed at its contents. There were all the usual male things including a can of shaving cream which, I noted, was not the brand he used on TV. He also had a pharmacy.

"There," he said defiantly. "Have you ever seen so much garbage? Codeine, amphetamines, vitamin B complex, Valium —that's a muscle relaxant, as opposed to Clyde's liniment, which is a muscle *soother*. More pain killers. And look at *this*. Nembutal, Seconal. Do you realize I could kill myself?"

Then, sensing perhaps that I had missed his point, he dove into the medicine cabinet and started all over again, describing each bottle's contents and how often he took them, while constantly monitoring my reaction. At last, with only the deodorant to go, he turned and demanded, "Who the hell needs this?"

I smiled. "Sammy Hines could have used it."

Mackin eyed me suspiciously. "What about Sammy Hines?"

"He was a running back, not a quarterback with the best protection in the league. He also happened to play long before they outfitted every jock with his own drug store. And when *he* quit, it was only because the doctors refused to operate again. How many times have you gone under the knife?"

Mackin blinked. "How do you know all that?"

"I grew up in Chicago." And had heard more about Sammy

Hines over dinner than I cared to know.

"Oh," he said. "Chicago." He looked at me curiously. And then, unaccountably, his mood changed. Gone was the churlishness, replaced by the engaging Mackin smile that had been absent all evening. The full two-dimpled version no less. His tone became teasing.

"Do people in Chicago believe you have to be a masochist to be a hero?"

"Do you really believe you're a hero?"

"Well, we all have our illusions. Though it's tough protecting them from female reporters. I'm tired."

I sat down on the edge of the tub. Mackin's game was wearing me out, too. And getting me nowhere. The man didn't want to tell me something and I couldn't think of one good reason why he should. Big deal. The world was getting weirder every day and I had to harangue a silly football player. I also, I reminded myself, had Maxwell to answer to, so I said, "It's going to come out in the end anyway. You know that."

"Lindsie," he groaned, "it's been coming out"—he checked his watch—"since *yesterday.*"

I smiled. "And you're so good at misdirection, Alex Mackin."

He rolled his eyes and leaned against the sink. "God, you're persistent. Don't you ever quit?"

"I quit."

"Good. Let's change the subject . . . will you marry me?"

I looked at the quarterback speculatively. "How do I know you don't just want me for my group medical insurance?"

Mackin grunted, looked around the bathroom. Glanced at the ceiling, studied the green wall-to-wall carpeting, snuck an occasional side glance at me. "Okay," he said abruptly, "get out your notebook."

Then, looking at me square in the eye, he said, "All my life,

Lindsie, I've been handed everything. I was always a good-looking kid, and since I was three I've been able to do anything in athletics I've wanted to. Everything's always come easily. I even did okay in school. By my third year in pro ball, the first year we won the Super Bowl, I knew I had it made. Check back, read up on what I did that season. You'll see. And it's been smooth as honey ever since. But the time comes when a man has to ask himself some tough questions. Like why? I've done everything I've ever wanted to. Set records, made a name, made money . . ."

"So you're bored?"

Mackin shook his head. "No," he said softly. "Not bored. Scared. It suddenly occurred to me one night there's only one way for this to come out right. I'm going to die. Probably soon."

"Oh."

I wondered what book he'd got that out of and then I realized it was just preposterous enough to be the truth. Especially coming from an athlete who spent the better part of each day fussing over his body. Still . . . Mackin was going to have to do a whole lot more to convince me that this was why he was going to retire from a football fortune, and at the moment, he was looking at me with those bedroom eyes . . .

It was a small bathroom in a disturbingly quiet apartment in the middle of the night.

So when the doorbell rang, I let out a silent sigh of relief. And followed him wearily down the hall.

I'm not that familiar with the San Diego Chargers, but the man who filled Mackin's doorway could only have been a defensive tackle.

He was a good six-and-a-half feet tall with a chest that I couldn't even begin to translate into inches. The nose had been flattened, though I couldn't imagine who would have dared,

26

and his stringy blond hair needed washing (though I couldn't imagine who would tell him). He wore a gray sweatshirt and a dopey grin and Mackin didn't look pleased to see him.

"Willy," he said. "Uh . . . come in."

Willy had already decided that was exactly what he was going to do, and as he entered the room I saw Mackin shrink before my very eyes. Next to Willy, he looked positively Lilliputian.

"Evening, Alex."

I saw then there was a second man. This one was all middle: middle-aged, middle-tall, and belly-middled. He wore gray slacks, yellow shirt, navy sport coat. Good clothes, badly worn. When you've got a gut like that, you don't hang it out for everybody to see, someone should have told him so. The rest he could do little about. The few strands of wispy black hair that remained, curled tightly about his large ears like mountain climbers clinging desperately to a rock.

Mackin closed the door after inviting the men to come in. None too happily either, I thought. He said, "Sam, Willy, this is Lindsie." We all nodded to each other and I wondered again, Willy who?

Mackin gestured for everybody to sit down and I found myself on the couch next to the man called Sam. Willy and Mackin sat in the leather chairs. After an awkward silence Sam said, "You boys sure played a fine game today, Alex. Knee didn't seem to bother you much."

"No," said Mackin, "not too much."

"It's a shame," the man went on, "they didn't take you out in the fourth period and let you rest up for the Super Bowl. Damn silly considering you could have been hurt."

Mackin shrugged. "It was only a fourteen point lead. Anything could have happened."

There was another long silence. Eventually Mackin said,

"Uh, would anybody like a drink?" He started to get up but Sam hurried to his feet and waved Mackin down.

"I'll see to it, Alex. Miss . . . ?"

"A light Scotch and water, please."

Willy said he'd have a beer and Mackin said he didn't think he wanted anything. After Sam had gone off to the kitchen, Mackin rolled his eyes at me and smiled. "Would you like to have lunch tomorrow, Lindsie?"

"Sounds good," I said, surprised. He had to know I'd only dump more questions on him. But then, maybe he wanted another chance to pitch me his death story.

"Where are you staying?"

"The Hotel del Coronado."

"You have a car?"

I nodded.

"Okay, there's a place downtown called True Grub. On Broadway across from the Westgate. About one?"

"True Grub?" I said. "What do I wear, smelly clothes?"

He grinned. "Yep."

After a while, Sam came out, fetched a bottle from Mackin's bar, and disappeared back into the kitchen. Eventually he returned and handed me a glass. Drinking on an empty stomach was probably dumb, but alcohol always made me feel full. And by then my stomach was making frightful noises.

After another awkward pause, Sam turned to me and said, "What are you, honey? A stewardess?"

Any stranger who calls me honey automatically loses points. "No," I replied, "I'm . . ."

"Aw, come on, Sam," said Mackin. "Don't insult me like that. A goddam stew, for chrissake."

Willy, who had been sitting bloblike in his too-small chair suddenly came to life. "Hey, man, you should have seen what was on the flight from Vegas. Right, Sam?"

Sam nodded disinterestedly.

"I mean she had knockers you wouldn't believe. And she didn't mind rubbing them against you either when she leaned over."

"Yeah, but you shouldn't have grabbed her like that," Sam said.

Oh, Christ, I thought. I continued working on the Scotch, which tasted like Chivas Regal, though a bit stronger than I would have fixed for myself. Mackin was fidgeting in his chair, looking faintly uneasy. And I wondered again who these creeps were.

Sam said, "So you'll be playing St. Louis in the Super Bowl, huh? I'll tell you Alex, they looked mighty strong out there today. That Sherwood—he's going to be tough. I wouldn't be surprised if you lost this one." He laughed.

"Oh," said Mackin. "You watched the game?"

"Sure. Watched both games over at Dion's. I'll tell you, Alex, it won't be like the game against the Cowboys."

Mackin looked down at his feet. "No," he said. "Probably not."

With Willy playing blob, and Mackin annoyed at being told he might not win the Super Bowl, Sam turned once again to me. He had small black eyes that were dull and humorless and there was something about him that made me want to scoot over to the end of the couch. "Is your drink all right, honey?" he asked.

I smiled. "Keep calling me honey. It really turns me on."

Sam gave me a stormy black look, which he then rotated to Mackin, who had laughed. "Better watch out, Sam, or she'll belt you with her roundhouse lib." He grinned and winked.

I giggled and reached into my purse for a cigarette. Refusing to be put off, Sam immediately leaned over and flashed his lighter, and as his jacket spread open, I stared. Black handle sticking out of brown holster. "Hold still," he commanded. I froze. "Or I won't be able to light it."

I sank back into the couch and looked at Mackin. He was talking to Willy but his eyes kept moving restlessly around the room. I put down my drink and stood up. And then, as Mackin's eyes grew wide, I sat down in his lap. It felt good.

"Honey," I murmured, breaking my own rule, "did you know that your friend Sam has a gun?"

The smile went out of his eyes as he glanced over my shoulder at Sam. "The problem," he said quietly, "is that you're too good a reporter."

"I've developed a fair eye for guns," I agreed.

"You got any good records, Alex?"

Mackin's eyes slid to Willy. "Yeah, man, go help yourself."

"Who are they?" I whispered.

Mackin grimaced. "Would you believe my bodyguards?"

"Your what?"

He ran his finger over my lips. "After all, my body needs lots of protection. Though right now, it feels pretty safe."

I straightened a bit. "Bodyguards?" I repeated. "What for?"

The room was suddenly rocked by no less than the *1812 Overture.* Mackin reached out for a strand of my hair and began gently tugging on it. "Tell you what," he said. "I'll tell you if you won't tell."

"Tell what?"

"There have been some threats on my life, stupid stuff, so the Chargers decided to assign me bodyguards until after the Super Bowl."

"But—"

"And the reason we're not telling anybody is that we don't want to give other weirdos any ideas." He paused. "Now I'm counting on you to keep this between us."

He said it in a deep husky voice, filled at once with both promise and suggestion. My head began to pound. I slid off his lap and nearly walked into the coffee table as I returned to the couch. The music was growing more furious and either the room was keeping time with it or I was getting slightly smashed. I sat down and decided I'd better wait a few minutes before driving back to the hotel.

Against the din came Sam's voice. "Another hopscotch?"

Mackin was smiling at me, his dimple running clear down his face.

"I'll bet you're a model," said Sam. I turned to look at him and over his shoulder I noticed one of the elephants eyeing me viciously.

"I don't like your elephants," I said. Mackin looked at me strangely and seemed to sink down in his chair. He was getting smaller and smaller, and soon he'd disappear through the little white door. "Don't go away," I said. "We're just getting to know each other." I laughed.

Willy said, "She looks like Royce's gallump don't you really, Sam?"

I looked back. The elephants were getting closer.

"Alex has a Rolls Royce," I put in.

"Not anymore. I traded it in on a porch."

"I like porches," I said.

Mackin laughed. And as the music crescendoed, I could hear the elephants' pounding footsteps. Mackin was still laughing . . . his mouth growing bigger and bigger. Closer and closer. And then, just when I thought he would swallow me, his mouth closed and his ears started flapping.

He reached out and hit me with his trunk.

Chapter 6

The sun was shining and a hippopotamus was peeking out from the trees.

I tried to get him to come to me, but he just stood there, his eyes half-closed, refusing to heed my desperate pleas. I cried out to him, shouting louder and louder and when I woke up there were tears on my face.

A wind kicked up and the trees began to sway, heavy white clouds rushing by overhead. I closed my eyes and when I opened them again, the trees had separated into single plants and the white clouds had solidified into a plaster ceiling. Slowly I raised myself up onto wobbly elbows, and even then managed to set off a grade ten earthquake in my head.

Sitting up, I rubbed my throbbing temples and blinked uncomprehendingly at the strange room until, once again, the hippopotamus grabbed my attention and jolted me out of my thick gray fog.

I moaned and sank back onto Mackin's couch.

A series of disconnected thoughts and images swirled through my head and I wondered vaguely how I could have been so stupid. To drink. I can't drink. The slightest bit of alcohol sends me embarrassingly to sleep, though not usually on someone else's couch.

The bamboo shades were framed with light, and I was surprised to find that it was approaching noon. That made me feel even worse. I never sleep till noon.

I got woozily to my feet and went staggering off in search of Mackin. He wasn't in the kitchen. I went back out, around the elephants, and through the second doorway leading down the hall. Bathroom door open, no one inside. His bedroom stood at the end of the hall; it also stood empty. I closed my eyes and groaned.

Little red hearts crawled all over the sheets and all over one entire wall. I fled back down the hall and paused at the bathroom door. Aspirin, I thought. In that medical arsenal surely he must have aspirin.

Naturally, he did not. At least none that jumped out at me from that jumble of bottles. "Whoever heard of not having aspirin?" I grumbled.

A flurry of little white labels swam before my eyes, refusing to sit still and identify themselves. Eventually the word codeine sorted itself out and I lifted the container off the shelf. Codeine. That's all it said. I shook out one white pill, debated, then decided I couldn't feel worse. I swallowed it down with a glass of water.

I closed the medicine cabinet and a wretched looking girl with tangled hair and dark smudges under squinty eyes peered back. I looked down. My dress was a wrinkled mess. I left the bathroom in search of my purse, and a comb, and as I entered the living room the doorbell rang.

Neat, I thought, and slowly pulled open the door.

She was tall and slender, strikingly pretty, and she looked disgustingly fresh. Skin of peaches and cream, clear hazel eyes, and lots of silky blond hair. The eager smile she had been wearing wavered, and after looking me up and down, vanished altogether.

"Oh," she said. "Who are you?"

"Er, hello. I'm Lindsie," I answered, which didn't help her much.

"Lindsie," she repeated and seemed not to like the sound of it. Her linen slacks bore not a single wrinkle and the jewelry she wore flashed expensively. "Well," she said, "may I please speak to Alex?"

"Er . . . he isn't here."

Her eyes narrowed in anger. "Of course he is," she said furiously.

I shook my head, carefully. "No. He was gone when I, uh, got here."

"Then where is he?" she demanded.

The sun was bright and shooting straight into my eyes. I leaned against the door frame. "I don't know," I said. And then, because that didn't seem to please her either, I added, "I'm the cleaning woman."

"The . . . cleaning woman," she said in a voice that clearly indicated she was certain I was not. "Well, you just tell Alex that Lisa was here."

She started to turn away, then paused. "You don't suppose it's his car again?"

I shrugged. "Uh, Lisa . . . ?"

"Lisa Lisle," she said through her teeth and more or less huffed away.

Ah, yes, of course. I recognized the name from several of the articles I had read on Mackin. Part-time model, part-time actress, and always identified as full-time "close friend" of Alex Mackin.

I closed the door against the glaring sun and found my purse on the coffee table. My hair hurt as I combed it . . . and then I stopped combing it altogether. True Grub. The name crash-landed inside my head. "Would you like to have lunch tomorrow?" When he had said that, tomorrow was tomorrow, but I had taken it to mean today. And it was now 12:35. I picked up my purse and went grubbily out the door.

True Grub was a small restaurant, dominated by a large bar in a part of downtown San Diego where you wouldn't want to walk alone at night. But aside from the address, there was nothing grossly grubby about the place, judging from the clientele. They were mainly men, mainly in business suits, and at this hour, mainly in the dining room.

The decor was Old West—wooden floorboards, dusky paintings of buxom women—and the maitre d' pure Gary Cooper. He strode over in his genuine leather boots and said he was genuinely sorry but there would be a fifteen-minute wait. I asked if Alex Mackin had come in, and he said, no, not today.

I began feeling woozy again and since the only free seats were at the bar, I wandered over and asked the cowhand tending it for a cup of coffee.

I held the cup in both hands and tried to make sense of the clutter of images and words that kept knocking around my head like dishes on a pitching sailboat. Hopscotch . . . Rolls Royce . . . angry black eyes . . . and great black voids.

"Excuse me, miss . . ."

I looked up with a start. Cowboy hat, sheriff's badge, worn leather vest. "Another cup of coffee?"

I noticed my cup was empty, but couldn't remember emptying it. Suddenly I realized a man was sitting to my right in a seat that had been vacant. I looked up at the big train station clock over the bar. One-twenty-five. Some 15 minutes had elapsed that I couldn't account for. I had simply spaced out.

"Miss?"

"Yes . . . another cup of coffee. And—could you serve me a hamburger as well?"

He said he could and I turned around on the barstool to scan the tables. But I knew at once that Mackin wouldn't be there. And if I hadn't been so befuddled, I would have known that before I had left his apartment. For it didn't make sense that he would go out, for whatever reason, and expect to meet me here, knowing the shape I was in. He would have either come back for me, or called. And even if I had missed him, he would surely have phoned the restaurant.

. . . Royce's gallump, don't you really, Sam? Something about a Rolls Royce. No, Mackin had said he had traded it in for a Porsche. Only he had said porch. Or had he? And those elephants. Why had they come off the wall like that? And they had, too, for I remembered thinking they were going to trample me; I had been truly afraid. And Mackin's dimples running down his face . . . Mackin growing smaller. Hallucinations, strange and scary.

My hamburger arrived and I started to bite into it, then I put it carefully down on the plate. Hallucinating. That's exactly what I had been doing. On one lousy shot of Scotch. True, I hadn't eaten since halftime at the game, when we were served sandwiches in the pressbox. That would have been . . . what? Two-thirty, three. And it was maybe twelve-thirty, one o'clock when I'd had the drink. But you don't hallucinate on one drink, I told myself. And even if I had, why would I still be so messed up?

I finished my hamburger and a third cup of coffee and drove carefully back to the hotel.

"San Diego Chargers, good afternoon."

"Bill Owens, please."

"His line is busy, will you wait?"

I said I would but had my doubts. It had been a hassle from the moment I had phoned the team p.r. man to get Mackin's unlisted number. He hadn't wanted to give it to me. And without actually saying so, he had made it clear he thought I was out to seduce the quarterback, if not the entire offense, and probably the odd safety or two. They were all like that, the p.r.

men, dead sure I was up to no good. Some were better than others. The better ones merely thought I was too dumb to write about football.

"Owens speaking."

"Hello, Bill. Lindsie Hollis."

Dead silence.

"About Mackin's bodyguards . . . "

"What bodyguards?" he demanded.

"The ones the Chargers assigned him until after the Super Bowl."

"What the hell for?"

I smiled remembering my very same reaction. "Alex told me there had been threats."

"Did he tell you when?" Owens said impatiently.

"Not exactly."

"The last threats against Alex Mackin were nearly three years ago," Owens snapped. "And at the time we did assign protection. But there's been nothing since. We go through all his mail, I'd know."

"You'd know," I said, "but maybe you wouldn't tell."

"Maybe not," he agreed, "but take it from me, there have been no threats and certainly no bodyguards."

"On the record."

"On the record, off the record. And by the way, when we do use bodyguards, it's always *on* the record."

"To serve as a deterrent?"

"Exactly."

I thanked him and hung up. Dialed Mackin's number and got no response. Thought. Mackin had asked if anybody wanted a drink and Sam jumped up to get them. He had walked behind the couch and into the kitchen, at least that's what I had presumed. But he could just as easily have gone through the second doorway and into Mackin's bathroom. Unless he had

brought something with him. But that didn't make sense because he didn't know I would be there. He had, I seemed to
remember, taken some time getting the glasses and ice before
going over to the bar for the liquor. So he could certainly have
gone into the bathroom and taken something out of Mackin's
medicine cabinet. But that didn't make sense either.

For why on earth would he have wanted to drug me—a
complete stranger?

Chapter 7

It was just after four when I walked through the wrought-iron gate and up to the front door. I pushed the top button.

"Yes?" answered a metallic voice.

"I'd like to speak to the resident manager, please."

The buzzer sounded and I pulled open the heavy oak door, crossed the Spanish tile, and paused outside the first door on my right. A shingle hanging above it said 'Resident Manager'. I knocked and was told to come in.

The voice belonged to a wide-eyed, pleasant-faced woman seated behind a large Mediterranean-style desk. She wore a bright yellow dress and an outdated yellow beehive hairdo. She appeared to be forty and, as I drew closer, spreading.

"Hello," I said. "Are you the manager?"

"I am. But I might as well tell you we have no vacancies." Then, fearing she had been too abrupt, "However, we might have something coming up in June."

I smiled. "Thanks anyway, but I wasn't interested in renting. I'm a friend of Alex Mackin's and I'm supposed to water his plants. He said I should pick up the key here."

"Oh." A small frown crept into her face, and a note of protectiveness into her voice. "Well, he didn't say anthing to me."

I worked up a giggle. "You know Alex," I said. "He's kind of forgetful sometimes."

"Don't I know," she declared. "I don't think that man has

_39_

once remembered to pay his rent on time. Though he's always so apologetic . . . " Her voice trailed off in dreamy memory.

I cleared my throat.

"Er, you say you're a friend?" Her eyes narrowed in grudging appraisal.

I nodded solemnly.

"I guess it will be all right," she said wistfully. "But don't forget to bring it back."

I unlocked the door and let myself into Mackin's apartment. It was deathly quiet, yet in the light of day, the jungle seemed less hostile, less like unseen eyes were watching. The plants were dappled with sunlight; the elephants, rather than looking sinister, seemed innocently caught in slow motion. The unspoken threat from the night before had, instead, taken on a new, more definitive shape.

On the coffee table sat one elephant tusk, one ashtray with two butts, mine, and one empty beer can, Willy's. Nothing more, such as my Scotch glass, which I'd come hoping to find. It had disappeared—and so had Sam's.

I wandered into the kitchen and switched on the light. A stack of grimy dishes rose tipsily out of the sink. Empty beer cans and Coke bottles overflowed the garbage pail. Unwashed pots littered the stove. No wonder Lisa Lisle hadn't believed I was the cleaning woman.

Not that Mackin had totally neglected his housekeeping chores. I walked over to the sink. And there on the counter, turned upside down to dry—two glasses.

So much for that, I thought, and returned to the living room. I sat down on the couch and pondered. Even forgetting the drinks, there was another problem. Where was Mackin? It was a Monday, the day after the AFC championship game, two weeks before the Super Bowl. Surely there had been no team meeting. But possibly Mackin had gone to see the trainer for

work on his arm or knee. I picked my way through the plants
and unraveled the phone. Brought it over to the coffee table
and, once again, dialed the Chargers' main office.

The receptionist said she'd be happy to give me the training
room number but everyone had gone home hours ago. If it
weren't for the barrage of calls concerning Super Bowl tickets,
she would have been long gone herself, it being New Year's Eve.

I interrupted the beginning of a sob story and asked for the
trainer's home number. I was a reporter, I said, on deadline, in
desperate need of a quick quote. She hemmed and hawed and
finally gave in.

A child answered on the third ring and went to find Daddy.

"Yes," said Herbert Willoughby. "Who is this?"

"Lindsie Hollis, Mr. Willoughby. I'm with *Monday* magazine."

"I don't have time," he said sharply. "We're just going out.
Dammit, Margaret, where's my other stay?"

I put a note of honey in my voice and assured him it would
take but a minute. And before he could protest, I inquired if
Mackin had been in that day.

"Alex? No. Why?"

"He didn't show up for our interview," I explained, "and I
was wondering if he might have been in, you know, because of
his knee."

"Nope. Wasn't in, and wasn't due in. In fact, if he followed
my orders, he should be up in the mountains right now."

"The mountains?" I echoed.

"Of course. Walking the hills is a fine way to strengthen a
weak knee. And it gives him a chance to get in some fishing."

"When do you expect him back?"

"Quite frankly," said Herbert Willoughby, "I don't expect to
see Alex until New Orleans. Sometime Thursday I should
think."

"Perhaps," I said slowly, "you might know where he is staying in the mountains?"

"Nope. It's a one-way street."

"I beg your pardon?"

"I don't need Alex," he said tersely. "He needs me. When he does he knows how to get in touch." On that final note, the trainer hung up.

I sat there chewing on my felt-tip pen. If he were going to the mountains, why had he invited me to lunch? And then there was Lisa Lisle. She, too, had been expecting to see Mackin. When I had said he wasn't home, she had replied, "Of course he is." Why of course? Because I had looked rumpled? Then she had something else. Something about, "You don't suppose it's his car again?"

My thoughts were getting tangled. Why had she mentioned his car? Because, I thought suddenly, she had seen it. Seen his car when she had arrived and naturally assumed he was home —unless something was wrong with his car.

I left the door unlocked and went downstairs and around to the front of the building. Under the first floor apartments were wide open archways leading into individual parking stalls. Cadillacs, Mercedes, a sports car or two—but only one Porsche. With California tags 777-MAC.

Back in his bedroom I studied the unmade waterbed. A black furry bedspread was crawling off it onto the floor, trying to get away, no doubt, from the red-hearted sheets, which were reflected in the mirrors on the closet doors. The whole room looked as if it had come down with a bad case of measles.

I began with the closets. Bill Blass's latest collection, and on the floor, scattered haphazardly among a dozen pair of shoes, were all those trophies I had been wondering about. But no crazy-colored running shoes. And no blue knit shirt.

I checked the drawers, picked through a wicker laundry basket. Several pairs of jeans, yes. But not the shirt and no nylon jacket.

Feeling even creepier, but hoping to find something helpful, I sat down at his desk and began riffling the drawers. The top one contained a mess of letters and a stack of snapshots. Mackin with Lisa Lisle. Mackin posing stiffly in front of the stadium. Mackin standing in the doorway of an apartment, holding a brown paper package and looking at the older man who had apparently handed it to him. Mackin lounging by a pool, hoisting a can of beer. There were no fewer than four bank books, two for savings, two for checking accounts. Guiltily I thumbed through them. Hefty balances in all.

I shuffled through the letters, studying the return addresses for mountain locations. But nothing. No Willy or Sam listed in his address book either. The other two drawers were crammed full of papers and cancelled checks.

I sat there biting my lip. Alex Mackin had made a lunch date with me, had seen me pass out on his couch, had left his apartment sometime before noon, presumably to go to the mountains, without finding out how I was, or leaving an explanatory note. Without changing his clothes or taking his car. Possibly in the company of two men whom he'd said were his bodyguards and who most probably were not.

You have to wonder, he had said, when do you pay up?

Chapter 8

"Goddam," said Tom Eastwick banging down his phone. "If I talk to one more faggot designer I'll start lisping myself."

"Like thith?"

"It's not funny."

I rolled the last sheet of paper out of my typewriter. Through the gap in the thin white curtains I could see the snow coming down like bits of wet Kleenex. "What are you working on?"

Disparaging eyes peered out from behind tinted aviator's glasses. "Mitchell's researcher is sick," complained Tom, "or more likely hung over. And I'm stuck with her story on the demise of the business suit."

"Again? I thought we suitably demised it two years ago."

"We did," said Tom with a faint grin. "But you know those people in Peoria. Sometimes we have to start trends twice."

His phone rang and I began rereading my memo to Maxwell. It was five double-spaced pages and covered three main areas: Mackin's paranoid death statement, a careful description of his two visitors and my reaction to the drink, also a brief summary of the following day's events. But before I turned it in to him I wanted to make a phone call, after Tom went to lunch. Eventually he pulled on his heavy wool jacket and said he'd be back in an hour.

I was just thumbing through my card index when my phone rang. "Lindsie? Doug Finney. Got a moment?"

I smiled and reached for a cigarette. Doug Finney was the

magazine's sports editor, a red-haired, freckle-faced man of thirty-five who took my forced intrusions into his beat with cheerful good humor, as he took most everything, including the world of sports. If other reporters were talking to the pitcher, Doug could be found interviewing the batboy. He had yet to cover a World Series or a Super Bowl, but he never missed a tiddly-winks tournament.

"I always have a moment for you," I said, and meant it.

"Then you're not going to turn me over for Mackin?"

"Well . . . it depends. How are your legs?"

"They may be better than his," declared Doug, "which is actually why I'm calling. I've picked up a few rumors, old girl. The gist is that the really big money won't touch the Chargers without points."

"The Chargers?"

"Right."

"But aren't they favored to win?"

"By five points, according to the published odds."

If you took the published odds, the game would start with the St. Louis Cardinals leading by 5 points . . . so a Charger bettor needed his team to win by 6. Yet, Johnny was telling me that the big, hidden money was demading just the reverse; they wanted the Chargers and 5 points, meaning St. Louis needed to win by 6 if their bettors were to collect. It was a bit complicated but what it boiled down to was somebody with a lot more information than me didn't think the Chargers could win by 6 points.

"Who told you this?" I said.

"Johnny Lee Lescano."

"The Las Vegas bookie?"

"Yes, well, I always put a few dollars down on the Super Bowl and . . . "

"Johnny favors the Cards?"

"No. He still likes the Chargers."

"Then what's the basis for the rumors?"

"He doesn't know. Only thing he can figure out is that something's wrong with Mackin."

I reached for a piece of paper. "Like what?"

"His legs maybe."

I winced. "Doug, you wouldn't have, by any chance, mentioned this to Maxwell?"

"As a matter of fact . . . "

I laughed.

"What's the matter?"

"Congratulations. You've just been promoted to one of his deep dark inside sources. Anyway, about his legs. He threw for three touchdowns Sunday."

"Yeah, but did you notice he didn't run even one option play? Usually Mackin options when he's down near the goal line."

"Still, as long as he can pass . . . "

"The Cards' defense is tough, Lindsie. They'll be going for Mackin every time."

"Then why didn't the Steelers?"

"Maybe their scouts didn't pick it up. Believe me, if something's wrong with Mackin it's not going to turn up in the NFL injury report. And according to Johnny a very few people seem to have some closely held information that's causing them to bet against the odds."

I said, "His legs seemed okay when I saw him. I mean he wasn't hobbling around or anything."

"Ran straight at you, did he? Oh, well, don't worry about it. I just thought maybe you could help me out."

I went downstairs to the vending room, bought a carton of milk and brought it back to my office. From my desk drawer I pulled out the rest of my lunch—an envelope of Carnation Instant Breakfast, chocolate, and three small bottles. I shook two vitamin C from one, a vitamin B from another, and a combination mineral pill from the third. I mixed the powder into the milk and sat there sipping it through a straw while popping pills. After a final slurp and gulp, I picked up the phone, asked for the Chicago tie-line and dialed my father's number.

"Lindsie!" he boomed in his fearsomely loud baritone, which undoubtedly scared the bejesus out of his players as it once had me. "What a nice surprise! How are you, honey?"

"Stuck," I said, "on a story about Alex Mackin."

"Alex?" he bellowed. "Hey, that's terrific." As usual, I had to hold the phone a full six inches from my ear. "And how is he? Jeez, did you see the Steelers' game? I'd give my entire offensive line for him."

"I think you might have to give your entire team."

"Now, honey, they're just a little inexperienced is all and we did have injuries . . . "

"Uh, Dad, I was hoping you could help me." The last thing I needed was another limb by limb dissection of his Bad News Bears. I had been getting their medical reports since third grade.

"Sure. Want me to put you in touch with anybody?"

"No . . . but maybe you could find out for me the exact condition of Mackin's legs."

I did not, in fact, know the exact condition of Mackin's legs. All I knew was his medical history, which I had used to bluff my way through the interview. It was always possible there *was* something wrong, and if there was, it would be top secret information. So secret that not even Johnny Lee Lescano would have it.

Dad sighed explosively. "Jesus Christ, Lindsie. Maybe you want their game plan, too?"

"I'd rather not," I said. "I hear it's going to have a tragic ending. The money's on the Cards."

"The hell it is. Who says?"

"Can't reveal my sources. When can you get back to me?"

"Later," he said grumpily. "By the way, what did you do New Year's Eve?"

"Flew."

"You?" said Dad incredulously. "You never get drunk."

"In an airplane. Home from San Diego."

"Lindsie, for God's sake, it was New Year's Eve. What about that lawyer fellow?"

I looked out the window for a moment and saw that the wet Kleenex had become lint and said with resignation, "I'm not exactly seeing him anymore. Look, I've got. . ."

"Why not?" Dad demanded. "Seems like a nice enough fellow."

"He is," I agreed. Nice and bright and brimming with visions of a future I didn't want to share.

There was a long pause. Dad was undoubtedly struggling with himself—as always, torn between playing parent or friend —and succeeding not very well at either. "You're almost thirty," he pointed out.

"Twenty-eight," I corrected.

"Your brothers were all married by the time they were your age," he reminded me. "People ask me about my children and I say I have three lovely daughters-in-law, five grandchildren, a daughter who thinks she's Brenda Starr and a goddamn parakeet named Fido."

"Spot," I said.

"A damn silly name for a bird," he grumbled. "Anyway, I'll see what I can do. And you might want to look up Chip for old times sake. He always was a sucker for you."

I laughed. "Dad, you don't miss a trick. I'll talk to you later."

I remembered the phone call I still had to make, thumbed through my card file, and dialed Peter Bent Brigham Hospital.

When I finally got through to Dr. Harold Solomon, I asked him what drugs, mixed with alcohol, could cause one to hallucinate. He asked why I was asking. So I told him briefly about San Diego.

"Alex Mackin?" he said excitedly. "What's he like?"

"Hal . . ."

"All right. It could have been the Valium or the Seconal. It could also have been a small amount of LSD. The first two generally don't produce hallucinations, but body chemistry differs and what affects one person may not affect someone else."

"Could I have hallucinated on Scotch alone?"

"I doubt it. It would have made you light-headed or giddy, but it doesn't cause elephants to come off the wall. Ten milligrams of Valium might have." He paused. "Then again, maybe it's all those vitamins."

"You're just jealous," I said. "You know I'll outlive you by twenty years."

"Maybe," he agreed. "But I'll be richer. You keep buying all those phony pills and . . ."

"I'll put all you doctors out of business?"

"You're hopeless," he sighed.

"That's a terrible thing for a doctor to tell his patient," I said. "Makes me want to drown myself in vitamin C."

He laughed. "Go drown. Call for me lunch sometime."

I said I surely would and hung up.

Later, as I sat trying to come up with a new lead for my muddled story, my father called back.

"I've got it on the highest authority," he began stentoriously, "that Alex Mackin's legs are not, repeat, not about to fall apart either now or in the foreseeable future."

"Who's the authority?"

"Herbert Willoughby."

"I see you went right to the top."

"Naturally. I told him I'd heard rumors that Mackin's knees might be going and if so, just between old friends, maybe they'd be interested in a trade. He said Harley Crittenden would trade his wife first."

"What did he say about Mackin?"

"Only that he twisted his right knee in practice last Friday, but nothing serious. That torn cartilage last season seems to have healed all right. So have his tonsils, which were removed when he was four."

"Dad, are you sure that's all?"

"My dear, the man is as healthy as a horse."

I lugged the Mackin file down into the Government Center subway and into the cramped car of five o'clock sullenness and pinched red faces and all the way through three screeching stops and two frozen blocks to my dark, empty apartment. It definitely needed another human occupant, but I didn't know who, so I fussed over my bird and let him out of his cage.

I peered out the frosted window onto Commonwealth Avenue, pitch black now but for the old-fashioned street lamps and the crawl of headlights along snow-packed streets. There was no way, I decided, I was going to run in that. So I changed into my sweatsuit and pounded out two furious miles on my exercycle and then I sat gloomily at the dining table watching Spot bully his toys and wondering how the hell I was ever going to write that story. The penguin thudded to the floor followed by the mirror and a teaspoon and then Spot.

"Such a bird," he blurted happily. And I said, yeah, right, and wondered again if Mackin were up to his old tricks or if maybe they had snatched him. But this was Wednesday and there had been no ransom demand, at least none that I knew of, and besides he had known them.

"Hi!" I felt a nibble on my right ear.

50

"Hi."

"Whatcha doin?"

"Thinking."

"What a mess!"

"You're right."

"How 'bout a kiss?"

"Okay."

"Extraordinary," said my bird and flew off to his cage.

So maybe he would show up in New Orleans after all and that would be that. And I'd look silly if I mentioned any of it in my story.

Then again, maybe he wouldn't.

I went down the hall to my study, a small, cluttered room filled with books, old newspapers, ancient files I would someday get around to throwing out, and a large messy desk. It also had a fireplace and a couch and a window overlooking a fire escape. A typical Boston Back Bay room. And it fit me like my favorite pair of jeans—at least it did when the heat was working.

It wasn't. I switched on my portable electric heater and sat down at the desk and thought a bit more about the whole thing. What Willy had said about the stewardess on the flight from Vegas and how Sam knew where the liquor was. Then I spotted my airline guide under the phone book and flipped idly through it and eventually called Maxwell. He would still be at the office.

"Yes, Lindsie."

"I want to go to New Orleans," I said.

A pause. "It's six-fifteen."

"There's a plane at nine."

"That's not the point," he said sharply.

"Well, I'd like to talk to some of Mackin's teammates. Our memo on Coach Sims, for instance, is pretty weak."

"Dallas is closer," he came right back. "We'll send someone out from there."

"No," I pleaded. "I need to talk to Mackin. I'll take my typewriter and file through Western Union."

Maxwell didn't even consider. "The story's botched up enough as it is."

"I'll unbotch it."

"I'm sure you will," he said smoothly. "From Boston."

I heard my voice rise. "No. I have to know what's going on or I can't write . . . Look, you know I never push this hard, I . . ."

Maxwell said nothing.

"Please?" It sounded inane.

Maxwell coughed. He always coughed when he was embarrassed. Perhaps he was afraid I would go emotional on him. He was like that.

"Sir . . ."

"All right," he cut in irritably. "But your story damn well better be the best thing I've read since the Bible."

"The Bible?"

"And call me in the morning."

"There's something else," I said. "It's not his legs."

"Oh?"

"He's healthy as a horse."

"Horses," said Maxwell, "are not necessarily healthy." I could already see the red pencil hovering over my still unwritten story. "Then how do you explain his retirement?"

"I can't," I said. "But if he does retire it won't have anything to do with his legs." Suddenly I saw all manner of legs. Thick gray legs pounding out of the wall.

"And the shift in odds?" Maxwell persisted.

It was possible, I thought. Anything was.

"Well?"

"It's not his legs," I said again. "The gamblers may have something better." I hesitated. "They may have Alex Mackin."

Chip Tobias used to say that if he could be anybody in the whole world he'd be Huckleberry Finn. And I always told him that was silly; Huckleberry Finn wasn't a real person. But Chip would just shake his head and say no, ole Huck was real all right. Else how come somebody wrote a whole book about him?

I thought about Chip as I watched the Mississippi River drift by, slow and thick and brown. He wasn't a whiz kid by any means, but in his own thoughtful way he usually came up with more right answers than most of us. "The important thing to remember is never let them know you're scared," he'd tell me when the boys were being mean. And one day I tried it and it worked and ever since I've never let anyone know that I'm frightened or worried. And I haven't cried either. At least not so as anyone knows.

Thinking about the old days made me remember the treehouse and Saturday afternoons at the movie theater with me stuck on the end and Chip, invariably, scrunched down on the other side. He was my youngest brother's age, two years older than I, and I had always liked him best. Probably because he was one of the few boys hanging around the house who had bothered to be nice.

I should have called him days before. It was just that I had no desire to go back. I had asked him for help so many times then, and now I needed him again. Things don't change.

"Lindsie, my God, how good to see you!"

I was too overcome to reply. It wasn't that he was squeezing me to death, it was all that itchy wool. "It's been what? Four years, five?"

I coughed and stepped back and said he looked pretty good to me, too, and then I wiggled my nose to make sure it hadn't been broken. I always forgot how big he had grown, or maybe it was just the bulk of his heavy white sweater.

"What are you doing here?"

"Come to collect my trading cards. Do you still have them?" It was a silly thing to say, I realized, but I suddenly felt awkward.

Chip laughed. "Of course I do. Along with all your drippy misspelled love letters."

"Oh, God, Chip. That's terrible!"

"Aw, I thought they were cute. Are you going to stand out here all day?"

He hustled me into one of the two chairs grouped in the corner of his room. There were two king-size beds but only one had been slept in. His playbook lay open on the other.

"So what's up, kid? Or did you just come down to see me win the Super Bowl?" He brushed the unruly strand of brown hair off his forehead just like always. He wasn't handsome, never had been. He had a long, narrow face with an aquiline nose. But he had those squinty brown eyes that always looked like they were laughing, and a crooked smile I had never been able to resist.

"I'm doing a story on Mackin."

"You are? Well, gee, Lindsie, he's not here."

I looked at the unmussed bed. "So I see. Anyway I talked to him in San Diego on . . . let's see, today is Thursday? Sunday night."

"And you didn't call me? Shame on—hey, hang on, here comes my food."

The bellboy wheeled in a table crammed full of ham, grits, rolls, juice, coffee, milk, and what appeared to be sixty thousand scrambled eggs.

"You're kidding," I said.

"Don't tell me you've forgotten? Here, let me dump this ham and you can have a plate."

"Plates give me heartburn."

"I've got Alka Seltzer. Eat."

We pulled up our chairs round the table and I took my time buttering a roll. I kept watching Chip and thinking how good it was to see him again. Every once in a while you get an ache to relive a certain day, and I guess if I had to pick one from back then it would be one with Chip in it.

"What kind of story?" he said through his eggs.

I tried pouring cream into my coffee cup. But it was one of those dumb pitchers and the cream went all over the tablecloth. "It's supposed to be about his retirement. Do you think he's serious?"

Chip stretched his mouth around half a dozen eggs. "You mean," he said swallowing, "he pulled that crap on you, too?"

The roll was stale. I reached for a serving fork and knocked over the salt shaker. "Then he's just doing one of his routines to get more money?"

"Sure. Hey, you remember the last time."

I did. Everybody did. It made the network news three weeks running. The high point in the contract negotiations came when Mackin called a press conference, piled the reporters on to a bus, and led them across town to "The Logan" area, where for two solid hours he tossed footballs with little Mexican-American boys. Asked why he was doing this, Mackin had solemnly replied that the cutback in federal aid to schools was depriving the kids of a good physical education program.

The dollars poured in from the charmed public, and it didn't take Chargers' owner Harley Crittenden long to read between the lines—of his accounting books, that is. Without Mackin the ending was neither happy nor profitable. Within days Mackin had his new contract. The terms were obscene.

"So how come he's not talking about it this time?" I asked.

Chip grinned. "Show biz, Lindsie. You've got to keep the folks guessing."

Well, he was sure succeeding at that, I thought. "And the bodyguards," I said, reaching for some grits, "are they part of the act, too?"

"Bodyguards?" said Chip.

"He told me . . ."

"Oh, come on, Lindsie. Don't believe everything he tells you. In fact, believe about half of it. Alex hasn't had bodyguards in years. Pass the butter?"

He smeared a roll and ate it in one gulp. I burst out laughing. "Our manners certainly have improved," I choked. "Remember how mad your mom used to get when we chewed with our mouths open?"

"And you used to say, 'But Mrs. Tobias, it tastes better that way'?"

"And you," I said laughing, "used to steal food off my plate?"

We ate and laughed and swapped remember whens, and I wished I could leave it like that and not dump all my questions on him. I waited until we were into second helpings before I steered the conversation back to Mackin. "Tell me, Chip," I said, "what's he like?"

Chip made a fist and brought it close to his mouth. "Alex Mackin," he said into his imaginary microphone. "One hell of a guy. Why, you know, Miss Hollis, there isn't a man in football who could keep this team of hotdogs together the way old Alex does. He knows when to joke and when to be tough and, just for the record, folks, he works harder than anyone."

"Even you?"

"Yes, ma'am. Every morning the son of a gun's out doing his three miles while old Chip's doing his z's." He unclenched his fist and looked down at his plate. "I don't know, Lindsie. I just don't have the same drive, I . . ." His voice trailed off.

I reached across the table and tapped his hand. "Come on, Chip. Aren't you the greatest white running back since Billy Clyde Puckett? You *make* Alex look good."

Chip smiled faintly. "Thanks, honey. More eggs?"

I nodded and he began telling me about his two little boys. I always thought it interesting that women talked about their husbands and men about their children. I tried to pay attention to Chip's but I kept wondering if the gamblers had Mackin— or he had me.

"More coffee?"

"Unless you'd like some."

"You really should have called us, Lindsie."

"I know." I took a sip of coffee. "Chip . . . does Alex ever gamble?" Maybe it had been nothing more than that.

"Gamble?" said Chip. "Hell, I don't know. He plays the horses some, who doesn't?"

"Is he friendly with any gamblers?" We were both eyeing the remaining dribble of grits. I beat him to it.

Chip seemed vaguely annoyed. "Christ, I doubt it. The league will fine you for that kind of thing. You get a little friendly with someone and they think you're going to dump a game."

"I suppose." My fishing expedition was floundering. I ate the last roll.

"Why Alex and I even got called in one year for something like that." He paused. "Do you always eat like that?"

I grinned. "Only when I'm with you. What happened?"

Chip ran his fork around his plate. "Maybe you heard about

it. The first year we played in the Super Bowl?"

"Not that I remember. What did you do?"

He yawned. "Oh, Alex and I were just sitting around the room one night when this guy calls up and asks if he can see us about some business deal. So Alex drags me out and we meet the guy and he takes us around in his Caddy for awhile. It was all kind of weird, but the upshot is he wants us to come in under the spread."

"That was the business deal?"

"Yeah. Some deal. He said he had Vegas dough behind him . . . naturally, they all say that. And all we had to do was win by less than ten and we'd make gobs of money."

"I suppose you get approached like that all the time," I remarked.

"We do," Chip agreed. "People just fooling around. Only this time we did come in under the spread and the league called us in."

"What did they do? Bug your room?"

Chip grinned. "Not quite. Seems one of the Cowboys had been having dinner in the same restaurant the next night and heard us laughing about it."

I said, "What did the league do?"

"Chewed us out for just joking about it. You know, like getting thrown off a plane for telling the stew you're going to commit hijack."

"And that's all?" The league was paranoid about things like that.

"Sure is. I shouldn't've even brought it up." Chip pushed back his chair and stretched his legs. "Now," he said with a smile, "tell me about you."

"May I smoke?"

"If it means you're through eating."

He went off to find an ashtray. I had debated telling him the story, I hadn't seen Chip in years, didn't know how he would react. I had figured it would have to be a last-minute decision. As he sat down and handed me the ashtray, I made it. I needed the reaction of someone close to Mackin. So I told him.

When I finished, Chip shook his head slowly. "I just don't understand," he said. "That doesn't sound like Alex at all." Then, skeptically, "Are you sure you were *drugged?*"

"Yes."

Chip shrugged. "Well I wouldn't worry about it. Probably Alex didn't know what that guy was doing."

"Maybe," I said. "Or maybe it's another one of his pranks."

"Don't be silly," Chip scoffed. "Alex isn't mean."

I looked out the window and noticed the Superdome a block away, squatting like a giant flying saucer that might take off at any moment. "But he does play games, Chip."

"Jesus, what's the matter with you?" Then, more reasonably, "Look, the kind of pranks he pulls are harmless. Silly little things to keep the guys loose or to give a reporter something to write about. Nobody ever gets hurt."

"Maybe," I said quietly, "he just went a little too far."

Suddenly, all the warmth went out of Chip's eyes. It had been too many years, I realized, and his loyalties had shifted, and I knew then I should never have come.

"What you don't seem to understand," he said distantly, "is that for all his shenanigans Alex is really a pretty straight guy. A lot of what he does is just covering up. He's built this kind of legend around himself as protection, to give himself breathing room. But underneath, he's a good man. Alex would never deliberately set out to hurt you, or anybody."

I said nothing. Uncomfortably, Chip played with his napkin. "Besides," he said looking up, "what would be the point?"

"I don't know."

"And neither do I."

The phone rang. Chip scooted out of his chair in obvious relief and answered it on the second ring. He spoke a few words, hung up.

"Bus is leaving for practice." He reached into the closet for his jacket. "How long will you be around?"

"Until Saturday," I said.

He picked up his playbook and together we walked down the hall to the elevators. As the doors opened, I reached up and brushed the hair out of his eyes.

He didn't seem to notice.

Back in my room I worked on the Mackin story, breaking from time to time to phone Mackin's apartment in San Diego and Lisa Lisle. I had managed to get her home phone number through her modeling agency. But neither she nor Mackin answered.

I sat at the desk and made faces at myself in the mirror and occasionally wrote a few sentences but I didn't like any of them. Finally I went back to the phone and called Doug Finney in Boston.

"I suppose you're stuck and need me to bail you out," he greeted me cheerfully. "I keep telling them girls can't write sports but nobody listens."

"Maybe you don't tell them hard enough," I suggested. "Anyway, how would you like to run down to New York for me this afternoon?"

"Sure," said Doug. "You need something from Bergdorf's?"

If I worked at *Monday* for fifty years I would never live down Bergdorf's. I had gone to New York for a story on a designer who had just come out with cellophane clothes, and in the course of the interview he had invited me to a private party that was being given in his honor that night. Black tie, of course. Since it was five o'clock when I left him and since Bergdorf's was just around the corner, I ran in and grabbed something off the rack. Naturally it showed up on my expense account and I have never heard the end of it.

"Not Bergdorf's," I said. "The secret files of the NFL."

"Oh, sure," said Doug. "That's easy. Are you nuts?"

"Probably," I agreed. "But so is the NFL. It keeps a file on approaches made to players by people who proposition fixes. And there was one made six years ago concerning the Chargers–Cowboys Super Bowl game. Mackin and Chip Tobias were approached. Can you find out what's in that report?"

"I'd rather go to Bergdorf's."

"There's that woman in NFL security . . . "

"Gretchen MacDougal. But why? Is it that important?"

"It might be. What I'm specifically interested in are names. I think the approach came from Las Vegas but I'm not sure. Maybe you could even get her to read it to you over the phone."

"Or better yet," said Doug Finney, "maybe I could just barge in with a submachine gun."

There are many things awesome about Alexander Mackin. The physical presence, to begin with, is overwhelming. The perfectly proportioned body is sculpted in taut muscles, the face ruggedly handsome, the charisma strong enough to make one female admirer sigh, "I bet even his sweat would smell good."

Then there is the way he performs on the field. That, too, is awesome. After nine years in pro football, Mackin holds more single-season passing records than any other quarterback. Twice this season, he led the Chargers to victory with performances that sent statisticians thumbing through record books and sports writers searching for superlatives.

Recently, the governor of California proclaimed Mackin's right arm one of the state's most valuable resources, and in Hollywood, a bidding war over the rights to his life . . .

I yanked the paper out of the typewriter, wadded it up, and shot it into the wastebasket. Then I went down to the lobby for a pack of cigarettes.

This job would kill me yet.

"Lindsie . . . Lindsie Hollis!"

I turned away from the newsstand and to three men walking across the lobby, one faster than the others. It was Fred Winkler from *Sports Illustrated,* I didn't know the others.

"Goddam," said Fred with feeling. "What's *Monday* doing in New Orleans on Thursday?"

"Waiting for Monday," I said. "How are you?"

Fred was a tall, bulky man about my age who always looked sloppy, complained about cholesterol, and grumbled a lot. He introduced me to his companions—his photographer and a reporter for *Time.*

"You look beat," I said to Fred.

"I am," he agreed with a heavy sigh. "I was just leaving St. Louis for San Diego and then I find out that idiot Crittenden has shipped his team here four days early." He eyed me suspiciously. "I suppose you've already talked to them all?"

"Not quite."

"Yeah, sure. The last time I ran into you we sat around drinking beer all day and I didn't see you do a damn thing. Then you ran that interview with Hassler and my editor says, 'How come she got that and you got one lousy quote?'"

"Was that your piece on Hassler?" asked the *Time* reporter. His name was Bob something. I told him it was.

"Yeah," said Fred. "You should see the way athletes talk to *her.* We're breaking our asses in the locker room and she gets taken to dinner and God knows where else. How many guys have you gone to bed with anyway?"

"You want it by team or just a rough estimate?"

Bob spoke up. "Come on, Fred. We'll be late."

"Where are you going?" I asked.

"To see Sims," Fred muttered.

"Is he holding a press conference?"

Bob shook his head. "He just agreed to see us up in his room for a few minutes."

They began moving toward the elevators. "Maybe," I called after them, "we could have a drink when you're finished?"

Fred turned back with a shrug. "Sure. Meet you in the bar in half an hour."

"Make it forty-five minutes," I said.

I sighed and wondered what was eating Fred. The few times I had run into him on assignment he had been friendly—even helpful. The interview with Hassler hadn't been a big deal. I had simply driven out to his house after the game and talked to him. Fred could have done that.

I went over to the reception desk and asked for a piece of paper. I wrote, "Lindsie Hollis from *Monday* phoned. Please call. Room 1221." I folded the paper in half and scribbled "Coach Sims" on it.

I handed it to the deskman knowing Sims would never call. Then I bought a magazine and sat down to wait.

Half an hour later, Fred and his two companions emerged from the elevator and turned left toward the bar. After they had gone inside, I rode the elevator up to the seventeenth floor. I found number 1700 at the end of the hall and knocked. Number 1700 was the slot the deskman had slipped my note into. After a moment, Coach Charlie Sims opened the door.

"Sir, I'm Lindsie Hollis from *Monday* magazine. I'm sorry to disturb you but I have only a couple of questions."

"I don't have time," said Sims inhospitably. He reached for the door.

"Well," I said, "I can't just print this thing about Mackin without confirmation."

The door hovered indecisively. Reluctantly it swung open. "What thing?" he growled.

Sims was a broad-shouldered man about six feet tall, wearing a black V-neck sweater over a white shirt and gray slacks. His brown hair was neatly combed. He would have had a nice-looking face if he hadn't been glaring at me. I said, "That Alex has been approached by gamblers to dump the Super Bowl game." I figured that would do for an opening gambit.

Sims just looked at me. "Why that's preposterous, Miss . . . "

"Hollis."

"Absolutely preposterous." He raised a large cigar to his lips.

"Then why have the Chargers assigned him bodyguards?"

Sims looked genuinely surprised but answered me with bluster all the same. "That's ridiculous," he snapped. "Nobody's assigned Alex bodyguards . . . I don't know where you're getting this crazy information."

"If Alex isn't being protected," I went on, "then why isn't he here?"

"If you'd done your homework, Miss . . . "

"Hollis."

" . . . then you'd know he's resting his knee." Again he began to reach for the door.

I stepped quickly inside. "He's not home."

Annoyance poured off his face. "Of course, he's not. If he were, he'd only be badgered by reporters like you." He made it sound like I was a plague.

"He's not in the mountains," I tried.

Sims opened his mouth to say something, thought better of it, and snapped it shut around his cigar.

"About his intention to retire . . . do you think he means it?"

"No comment."

That surprised me. I figured he'd say of course not. "You

mean," I said, "you're about to lose the best quarterback in football and you have no comment?"

"Honey, I've got a Super Bowl to put on," he said condescendingly, "and he'll be here for that and right now that's all I'm concerned about." He tapped a long ash onto the rug. "If you'll excuse me now, Miss Hollins."

"Hollis. Just one more question, sir. Did Alex actually tell *you* that he won't be back next year?"

Sims looked at me frostily. "Why ask me? If you're so concerned about it, why don't you ask *him* if he intends to retire?"

"Well . . . I did."

"And?"

Sims' face was impassive. But not so his eyes. For one brief moment they looked almost haunted. "You really don't know do you?" I said softly.

"No, Miss Hollister, I don't."

I joined Fred and the others in the bar hoping to find out if they knew anything about Mackin's retirement or nonappearance that I didn't. Nobody seemed concerned that he hadn't shown up. Fred and his photographer agreed that Mackin would not retire; Bob thought he would.

"It's different this time," he said. "I was talking to him before the Steelers' game and he told me he was just plain tired. That it was hard for him to get up for a game anymore. And that he was fed up with the whole rigmarole. People making demands on him all the time. He said it was funny that so many people assumed he led the perfect life. He said nobody had any idea how tough it was. And you know?" Bob ran his finger around the rim of his glass. "I believe the guy."

Walter Cronkite was doing his best to fill the half-hour. But it was Thursday, January 3, and America still had the post-holiday blahs. It would be a good week before the crazies and the politicians got cranked up again. I was just reaching to switch him off when the phone rang.

"Lindsie? Doug. Lunch at the Ritz at the very least. You got a pencil?"

"Hang on."

I got my pen and notebook from the desk and sat down on the bed. "Okay."

"I've got to give it to you fast because I'm at LaGuardia. On the Thursday before the Super Bowl game Mackin and Tobias were approached by a man who called himself Mr. Smith. He said he represented a group of businessmen, didn't say where from, who wanted to invest some money on the game. He said the published odds had the Chargers winning by ten and all Alex and Chip had to do was keep it under that for fifty thousand bucks."

"Apiece?"

"No, to split. According to Mackin they were being driven around in a limousine and it was getting close to curfew. They didn't want to be late so they told him fine. But apparently he never got in touch with them again and they figured the guy had been half looped."

"And the NFL let them off just like that?"

"No. They looked over the game film pretty carefully. Mackin got sacked halfway through the third quarter and sat out most of the rest of the game. He'd already thrown two touchdowns and when he came back in he nearly threw another. The League couldn't find anything wrong with that and cleared them both after telling them, I quote: 'You are officially pardoned by the commissioner's office for foolish, and what could have been damaging conduct to the National Football League. But you are not absolved of all blame. Any future transgressions of this nature will be dealt with most severely, up to and including your permanent suspension from the League.' "

"Would you be reading from a Xerox copy?" I said.

"Certainly not. I used my James Bond pocket camera."

I laughed. "Lunch at the Ritz then. And Doug . . . thanks."

Something was bothering me, but I couldn't think what and then the phone rang again. It was Chip.

"After that breakfast," he declared, "you owe me dinner."

"This isn't my day for cheating on expense account," I said. "Lunch at the Ritz and now dinner for you."

"The good news is I'm starved."

"Could you maybe fill up on beer and peanuts first?"

"Yeah. Come on up and we'll have cocktails."

"No Alex?"

"Not yet."

I looked out the window at the Superdome hovering ethereally in the night. And suddenly I knew what was wrong.

"Are you still there?"

"Yes. Er, Chip?"

"Hm?"

I had to ask him then because I couldn't do it face-to-face. I didn't want to do it all. "Chip . . . is there any possibility at all . . . "

"What?"

" . . . That Alex could have fixed that game without your knowing it?"

I waited for the explosion. Waited for what seemed forever. And when he finally answered it wasn't with anger, but worse, sadness. "You know," he said quietly, "I still remember you from the old days. A tall, skinny girl with great big eyes and pretty long braids. A sweet little girl without a mean thought in her head. What's happened to you, Lindsie?"

"You didn't answer my question," I said softly.

"I didn't think I had to. There's no way in hell Alex would ever throw a game. Is this what we're going to talk about all night?"

"I won't say another word."

"Then you can take me out on the *Miss Lucy.*"

"The who?"

"It's an old Mississippi riverboat that's been restored." He paused. "I thought . . . "

I smiled. "I know, Chip." Things don't change.

Chapter 10

Mackin still had not shown up the next morning.

"They're pretty pissed," Chip told me over the phone as he was leaving for practice. "I think they're going to call Crittenden if he's not here tonight. They want to give him the benefit though, because Crittenden will have his ass."

I asked Chip to call me if Mackin showed up. Then I tried Lisa Lisle's number once more.

"Hello?" said a sleepy voice.

"Miss Lisle?"

"Yes?" I heard a yawn. "Who's this?"

"I'm Lindsie Hollis, a reporter for *Monday* magazine. I'm sorry if I woke you."

"If it's about Alex . . . " she began angrily.

"I'm afraid it is. I'm the cleaning woman you met the other day." I paused. "Only, of course, I'm not."

There was a long grudging silence. Then, "What do you want?"

"I need very much to talk to you, Lisa. Perhaps you'd like to make a cup of coffee and call me back." I gave her my number at the hotel and waited while she found something to write it down on.

"Is he . . . there?" she asked hesitantly.

I drew in a long breath. "No."

Fifteen minutes later she rang back. I had been trying to figure out how to explain my presence in Mackin's apartment without really explaining it. But nothing brilliant came to mind. I would just have to fudge it.

"What do you want to talk to me about?" she said warily.

"First I'd like to apologize for the lie," I told her. "It's just that it was so embarrassing. Nothing like that has ever happened to me before."

"Nothing like what?" she said skeptically.

"You see," I began, "I had dropped in on him after the game to ask him a few questions for a story we're doing. And while we were talking, two guys showed up. Someone named Willy, a huge blond guy about six-six, and a bald-headed man named Sam."

"Willy and Sam?" she repeated. "I don't know them."

"You're not missing anything. Anyway, Alex said he was sorry the interview had been interrupted and maybe we could finish it over lunch the next day. He mentioned a place called True Grub."

"Unhuh. Alex goes there a lot."

"Well this is the embarrassing part. We started drinking and . . . well, I passed out."

"Oh, really?"

"I hadn't eaten since lunch," I went on, "and I guess I had too many Scotches. You can imagine how embarrassed I felt when I woke up the next morning on the couch."

"The couch," she repeated.

"And he was gone. And then you came."

"That's very nice," said the cold, distant voice. "And now I suppose you're wondering why Alex never called you again?"

"Lisa," I said, "believe me, I'm not interested in Alex. I'm interested in getting my story done. And he didn't show up at True Grub. The article's due in a couple of hours and I simply have to reach him. I'd really appreciate your help."

"I have no idea where he is," she said bitterly. "We were supposed to go out New Year's Eve but he never came by." She paused. "I thought he was with you."

"But surely he's told you since then . . . "

"No. I haven't seen or heard from Alex since right after the game." She hesitated. "It's just not like him to break a date without calling."

"His trainer said he sent him up to the mountains for a few days," I offered.

"Maybe he did. Alex didn't say."

"Do you know where he might be staying?"

"No. Alex takes off all the time without telling me. Every spring he just disappears and God knows where he goes."

"Disappears?"

"I don't know what else you'd call it. He closes up his apartment and cuts off the phone and says I'll see you, Lisa. He's been doing it for five years."

I remembered then reading something in the files about Mackin's off-season vanishing act. But I hadn't realized it was that complete. I said, "And nobody knows where he goes?"

"No. And then one day in July he'll call up and start talking like we had seen each other only yesterday. He used to get mad when I asked, so I don't anymore."

"But wasn't he in Africa last year?" Surely she had seen the photographs.

"For a month, I think. I don't know where he was the other five."

It didn't sound like a particularly happy relationship for Lisa Lisle. I wondered why she even bothered. I said, "Well, thanks anyway."

"Wait a minute," she cut in. "You told me he wasn't there yet. Isn't he supposed to be?"

"Apparently he's not due for another day or so," I lied. "Unfortunately my deadline's now. Sorry to have bothered you, Lisa."

After disconnecting I phoned down to room service for another pot of coffee. I had been up since 5:30 writing and at last I was nearly finished. It would be a typical *Monday* cover story, long on color and anecdotes, and filled with those mindless details that Maxwell demanded—what Mackin wore, how much juice he drank for breakfast, the kind of car he drove—most of which I had culled from the lengthy memo Al Larkin had filed from our Los Angeles bureau.

Mackin's retirement I handled by posing as the great question gnawing all of footballdom . . . and never really answering it. I wrote not one word about his latest vanishing act. I figured that if he didn't show up by Sunday morning, I could dictate a brief insert.

The coffee arrived and I sipped it while finishing off the last few takes. Then I called Maxwell to tell him the story was on the way.

"I'm sorry, Lindsie," said Marianne, his efficient, Swedish-born secretary, "Mr. Maxwell's in a meeting. Could you call back in half an hour?"

I said I would and went down to the lobby to pick up the morning papers. I was just heading back to the elevators when I ran into Bob Atwood, the reporter for *Time.*

"Hi," he said cheerfully, "how's your story coming?"

I smiled. He looked as frazzled as I, in his rumpled sweater and jeans. I was glad to see someone else was suffering; I always thought it was only me.

"I just finished it, thank God."

"Lucky you."

"When's your deadline?" I inquired.

He grimaced. "Today. Only I'm hung up on this Mackin thing."

"What Mackin thing?"

"His not being here. It's really put me in a bind because I was supposed to interview him last night and file this morning."

"I thought you talked to him last Sunday." I said.

"Only for a few minutes. And I don't know how the hell to reach him. The Chargers won't tell and when I called Crittenden he said he knew where Mackin was but wasn't going to say."

"That's nice," I said.

"And typical," he added. "Ever since we ran the story on Crittenden he's been no friend of ours. He's a real head case that man."

I laughed. "I think all owners are, Bob. I don't know if they start off like that or football makes them that way. Anyway, you have my sympathy."

"Thanks. Maybe we can have a drink later." He made a face. "Christ, I hope they don't send me back to San Diego."

"Me, too," I said and meant it.

When I got through to Maxwell, I told him the story was on the way.

"Fine. Any problems?"

"Only that he isn't here yet."

"What does the team say?"

"Not much. I don't think they know what to think. Of course it's interesting that Lisa Lisle hasn't seen him all week."

"Who the hell is Lisa Lisle?" Maxwell grumbled.

"Mackin's girl friend. He never showed up for their date New Year's Eve." I hesitated. "Sir, I'd like to go back to San Diego."

"Goddam," Maxwell exploded. "We're not running a travel agency. You'll do nothing of the sort."

"If Mackin doesn't show or something's happened to him we'll look pretty ridiculous," I pointed out.

Maxwell sighed. "Lindsie, the man is twenty-four hours late. The Chargers aren't worried, why should you be?"

"You didn't read my memo."

"Of course I did. And I don't like it. But that still doesn't prove something has happened to him. Anything else?"

"*Time* magazine's worried."

"What's that got to do with it?"

"They're doing a cover, too, only Mackin didn't show up for his interview." I paused and lit a cigarette. "I think they have some information because they're sending a guy to the West Coast." Or might, I thought anxiously.

Maxwell didn't respond. I could imagine him sitting there drumming his fingers on the immaculate glass-topped desk, then rubbing away the smudges. "I'll put Larkin onto it," he said abruptly. "And you . . . stay put. Call me later after I have a chance to look over your story." He hung up.

I sat there brooding. I didn't want Larkin on the story. I didn't want *Time* on the story. I wanted me on it. It was my story and now I was going to lose it.

I sighed and took my neatly typed pages down to the fourth floor, where the NFL had set up press facilities. I told the Western Union man to send it day press rate right away. Then I sulked back up to my room.

I began pawing through the jumble of papers, notes, and news clips strewn about the bed and floor until I finally dug out my scribbled notes from Mackin's little party. I had been over them a dozen times, trying to reconstruct everything that had been said. I began working them over once more.

" . . . You look like a model . . . She looks like Royce's gallump . . . " I flipped through the unintelligible phrases until I reached the beginning. I read it all through and still I couldn't find anything helpful. I picked up a pen and began writing. Mackin had seemed surprised when the doorbell rang, definitely not pleased to see the two men. Yet they hadn't apologized for the intrusion. Mackin invited us to sit down and Sam said something about the game. Then Mackin offered us drinks and Sam went to get them. He obviously knew his way around

Mackin's apartment. And he knew right then he wanted me drugged. Why? And why couldn't he have waited to see if I'd leave?

Answer: He didn't know I was a reporter and may have assumed I'd be spending the night. I thumbed through my notes again. Something about the Super Bowl was said. Something about Sam watching both NFL playoff games at some place called Dion's and that the Cards had looked tough and he wouldn't be surprised if the Chargers lost. Okay, fair enough. Though most people would have given the Chargers the edge, it was a conversational enough thing to say.

But there had been something else. Something about, "It won't be like the game against the Cowboys."

At the time I had taken it to mean the Chargers' trouncing of Dallas late in the season. But now I wondered. Couldn't he just as well have been referring to the Super Bowl game six years ago, the one Chip had told me about? It would, I decided, have fit the context of the conversation better.

I put down my pen and began repeating the sentence aloud, as if someone were speaking it conversationally. Still, no matter how I phrased it, it could have been meant in one of two ways.

Either Sam was telling Mackin that he'd have no choice this time. Or he was saying, this time, Alex, it won't be as easy for you to insure our odds.

And Lisa Lisle had said Mackin had been disappearing every spring for five years.

I reached for the phone and made one quick call. To reserve a seat on the next flight to San Diego.

Chapter 11

It looked like a moldy sundae. Filthy whipped topping afloat on a bowl of rancid chocolate ice cream with a few green sprinkles poking out. Then the plane swung over the Pacific and turned left toward San Diego. Los Angeles disappeared into its smog.

I glanced at my watch and figured in the two-hour time difference. By the time I rented a car and drove out there, it would be too late. I'd have to postpone it till morning. Which was all right, because I had another stop to make first.

I hurried up the circular drive to the front door of Mackin's apartment complex. I rang and was buzzed in, and once again I presented myself to the woman in the rental office.

"Oh," she said frowning. "It's you again."

"The plants . . . " I began.

"Of course," she said coldly. "You're here to water Alex's plants." She made it sound indecent.

"It's been several days," I said.

She looked pointedly at her watch. "I'll be leaving shortly. Will you be long?"

"Fifteen, twenty minutes, I should think. He's got a lot of plants."

"So of course you'll be back."

"I beg your pardon?"

"To water his plants *again.*" The key was gripped tightly in her hand.

I stepped up to the desk and gently tugged it from her reluctant fingers. "Maybe," I said. "But probably not."

"Oh?"

"Alex and I had a quarrel." Her large gray eyes lit up in hopeful expectation. "Over his coleus. But I pinched it back anyway. He'll be furious. But you can't just let a big beautiful coleus go to seed, can you?"

"Er . . ."

"And the way he treats that poor battered Boston fern." I sighed. "Maybe you could talk to him sometime." I smiled. "I'm sure he'd listen to you."

She nodded in confusion and hardly seemed to notice when I closed the door behind me. I spent about fifteen minutes going through Mackin's desk. And sure enough it was there and I felt my stomach get all knotted up because it wasn't supposed to be that kind of assignment. Just find out why the big-deal football player is retiring or not retiring and go on to something else. Now I had this mess on my hands.

I stood up and reached across the desk to switch off the lamp. And that's when I noticed it lying on the bed. His blue knit shirt. I stepped over and picked it up and knew it hadn't been there before.

I went through the rest of the apartment then, searching for other signs that Mackin had been home. His toothbrush and electric razor were still in the bathroom. In the living room, the empty beer can remained on the coffee table. And in the kitchen, the same mess.

I picked up an empty Coke bottle, filled it with water, and went to see to his plants.

The first thing I did after checking into a hotel was to phone Chip. And the first thing he told me was that Alex Mackin still had not arrived.

"Has he ever been late before?" I asked.

"Never," said Chip. "Alex is always on time. *Always.*"

"Isn't anybody worried?"

"Just me. Everybody else is pissed off. Sims is trying to get through to Crittenden. But if he doesn't know where Alex is I'm going to say something. Want to have a quick drink?"

I told Chip I was in San Diego.

"Have you tried Lisa Lisle? She might know."

"She doesn't," I said. "But what about where he goes during the off season. Does he have a place somewhere?"

"You got a snorkel with you?"

"Oh come on, Chip."

"No, really. Alex is into marine biology. He's trying to save the ecology or something. I think he works for the Scripps Institute."

"You mean when he isn't playing Dr. Livingston?"

"Well you can't expect him to just sit around all winter. God knows, he doesn't have to work."

"Ecology?"

"You got it. Call me tomorrow."

I hung up and tried to picture Mackin studying underwater vegetation, but all I could come up with were visions of droopy plants. Then I sat there trying to steel myself for the next call, to Maxwell. It would be just after eleven in Boston, but being a Friday night, I knew he wouldn't have gone home yet. I also knew he would be furious.

"San Diego?" he repeated in disbelief. "California?"

"Yes, sir, I—"

"Dammit, Lindsie, what the hell is going on?"

"You wanted to know why the big money wasn't betting on the Chargers? I think I'll have the answer for you tomorrow."

"Tomorrow?" said Maxwell incredulously. "And just how many tomorrows do you think we have? The goddamn Super Bowl is nine days away. Maybe you want to run an advance story *after* the game?"

I began to get angry. I had done a good job for *Monday* magazine for four years and you'd think that for once they might go with you. They told you to dig, never leave a stone unturned. Get all the facts and get them right. And then when you tried, they wanted to know why the hell you were joy-riding around the country, piling up expenses, missing deadlines, messing up their carefully formulated routine. They had it all figured out and couldn't comprehend when someone couldn't see you *this* week, when some stories didn't pan out, when others took off in unexpected directions. Sitting in their glassed-in offices atop the city of Boston, they expected the entire universe to fall neatly into their carefully laid-out pages. Well to hell with them and to hell with Maxwell, too.

"If you'll kindly let me explain," I said sardonically.

"On Tuesday," he said harshly. "Ten o'clock."

He was probably already calculating the long distance phone bill. I took room-service menu off the desk and studied it.

"Now about your story."

"All right."

"You say Mackin gained 2,358 yards passing this season. Tom checked the NFL records and they say 3,258. Can you check that, please?"

"Tom's right," I said automatically. "It must have been a typographical error."

"Also, you say Mackin drives a purple Porsche. That isn't good enough."

"It should be," I said dryly. "It cost $14,000."

"How do you know that?" Maxwell demanded.

"It's a Targa 911."

"Then you should have said so. You're getting sloppy on details, Lindsie."

I said nothing. I could see him reaching for his black book

and adding a couple dozen more checks after my name. Maxwell kept a very accurate accounting.

"You also," he went on accusingly, "make the statement that
Mackin's never been healthier. But you don't attribute it. We
need a name."

"No name," I said. "That came from my father who talked
to someone in the Charger organization. His credentials on the
subject are impeccable but he didn't know he was talking for
publication."

Maxwell droned on like a prosecuting attorney. I continued
studying the menu. Spanish melon or fresh-squeezed orange
juice? No, not fresh-squeezed. I dug a pen out of my purse and
carefully printed 'ly' over the hyphen.

At last he said, "Where are you staying? The Westgate?"

The faint sarcasm didn't escape me. I wiggled my toes inside
my shoes. Then I thought, screw it. "That's right," I replied.

"Fine," said Maxwell. "Add that to your bill. And Lindsie?"

I sighed. "Yes, sir?"

"If Mackin turns up in New Orleans tomorrow, you damn
well better be first in line to see him."

I started to protest.

But Maxwell had already hung up.

**Chapter 12**

I have a special coin in my wallet. I don't even know how it got there. But every now and then I dig it out. On one side it reads, "Forget It." On the other, "Do It Now."

The light was beginning to change outside my window and the traffic seemed to be picking up. Ten flips. Six Do It Nows. Four Forget Its. Weak odds . . .

So Mackin had been home again. Maybe the guys _were_ gamblers. Maybe they had taken him off to Las Vegas for a more provocative New Year's Eve than Lisa Lisle could provide. Maybe he had a great uncle in San Francisco who had died and left him money. We all screw up once in a while.

. . . But not me. You learn to read between the lines and behind the eyes. You get gut feelings. And mine had never been that far off. I reached for the switch on the bedside table and slid back under the covers.

Maxwell could fire me for disobeying orders. But he wasn't going to get me for being wrong.

"Miss Hollis?"

I glanced quickly up from _The Care and Treatment of Torn Cartilage, Volume Two_ and found a tall, slender woman standing over me. Her sleek black hair was secured firmly in a knot at the back of her neck, her skin was flawless, her eyes questioning. I tossed the journal back on the table, stood up, and said I was.

"I'm Elaine Hernandez, Mr. Crittenden's executive assistant. May I help you?"

Oh Christ, I thought. I had figured they would send out someone from further down the hall.

I said, "Is he in?" and tried to size her up. Cool, efficient-looking, a woman undoubtedly capable of dealing with passes from players and histrionics from owners, not to mention the outbursts of her own schizzoid boss.

"I'm sorry," she said formally. "Mr. Crittenden isn't here at the moment. Perhaps I can help."

"Of course," I said quickly. "I've only come to see a game film." It wasn't much of a reception room. The blue carpeting was indoor-outdoor and dirty. The walls were painted a wretched shade of gold and hung with pictures of Chargers in action. The centerpiece seemed to be a seven-foot-high trophy case crammed with team honors.

"I'm afraid that isn't possible," she said firmly. "You need authorization first. Unfortunately everybody's in New Orleans . . . unless you'd like to come back."

"I can't," I said flatly. "I'm past deadline as it is." I smiled. "I'm sure there won't be any problem."

She smiled back. "I'm sure there won't . . . once I check with Mr. Crittenden."

I decided I'd better get angry. "But that's ridiculous," I snapped. "I've never run into this kind of nonsense before. All this red tape for a silly old game film?"

She stood very straight, regarding me with slightly raised eyebrows. "Just how old, Miss Hollis?"

"The Super Bowl," I said with a sigh. "Between the Chargers and Cowboys."

"Why that one?" purred the cool, unruffled voice.

I furnished a look of exasperation along with the first thing that came into my head. "Because," I said, "Alex told me it was one of his finest games and I wanted to mention the highlights in my story. You do realize, Miss Hernandez, this is for next week's *cover?*"

A small patient smile. Wasn't about to take it personally. Nor was she about to budge. "I understand," she replied calmly. "But you'll just have to come back. We've had some problems with unauthorized personnel getting into the office."

"Then why don't you just authorize me? I mean you're his executive . . . "

I stopped. She had said assistant, not secretary. It struck me that Crittenden was hardly the type to hire a beautiful executive *assistant.* The title would have been her idea. I began backing off.

I smiled sheepishly. "I'm sorry . . . please forgive me. I guess I tend to overreact when it comes to football. I suppose it's all those hassles I always have. I'm afraid I've become paranoid, Ms. Hernandez. In fact, I was just thinking that if Al Larkin had come down from L.A., he could have walked right in and . . . " I left the sentence for her to finish.

She seemed to relax ever so slightly. "Yes," she agreed, "he could have. But that's because we know him." She pursed her lips thoughtfully. "If only you'd arranged this ahead of time."

I said nothing. The laws of psychology often parallel those of physics. It's harder to move an inanimate object than an animate one. If I came right back at her she would find it easier to bat me out the door.

She bit her lip, considered, decided. "May I see your credentials?"

I dug out my wallet and flipped through to my press card. "And it's just the one game film?" she said glancing at it.

"I know how to work the projector."

She laughed, nodded. "I'm sure you do, Lindsie, come along."

I followed the orange wool dress and long brown legs through a door, down a curving blue carpeted hallway and past the untidy offices of club executives and coaches. Like the titles on the doors, the offices grew fancier the farther we walked. I did a double-take as I came up on the one marked General Manager. The walls were tangerine. At Crittenden's door at the end of the hall, I stopped cold.

Elaine Hernandez, who had started in through the door adjacent, turned round.

"Pigskin *wallpaper?*" I said.

She nodded resignedly. "I'm afraid so." She came up a step. "Actually he wanted to use players' hides," she whispered, "but the coaches talked him out of it."

It sounded like a worn joke but I smiled anyway and followed her into a small, rectangular room. Oilcloth covered the windows on the far wall, and facing into each of the side walls were a desk and film projector. "Two of the assistant coaches share this office," she said and gestured for me to sit at the desk on the right. She left momentarily, returned with a key, and unlocked a closet.

I sat down and watched her search it. There seemed to be hundreds of films, all neatly aligned on the shelves. Under lock and key. Talk about paranoia.

At last she emerged with a reel of film and moved efficiently about the room, pulling down the screen from the wall in front of the desk, threading the spool, shoving aside papers. I couldn't help remembering all the times I had watched my father doing the same in our den at home.

"It's all set," she said straightening. "I have to get back to work. Just call me if you need anything." The lights went out, the door behind me closed.

I leaned over and switched on the projector. Like most NFL films, this one was black and white with no sound. It had been shot in typical game film fashion, with a single camera positioned in one of the upper decks. The cameraman held wide to show all the players, stopping the camera after each play and starting it up again as the offense reached the line of scrimmage. To anyone used to watching football on TV, the film would appear disjointed and confusing because there were no fancy cutaways, no continuity. But from all those sessions at home, I knew how to read between the frames.

The Chargers had apparently won the coin toss and elected to receive. They took the kick on the five and ran it back to the twenty-seven. The first drive went as easily as if they diagrammed it. Mackin ended it with a neat 33-yard touchdown pass to Hilton Jones, his wide receiver.

I lit a cigarette, settled back in the chair, and began scribbling notes. Mackin looked good, no doubt about it, and I found myself watching him with fascination. It was the way he moved. The absolute control over his body. The quick feint to his right, the slow graceful step back. It wasn't so much what he did with a football, but the purity of motion. It was disturbingly sensual.

The Cowboys had trouble moving the ball in the first quarter. It wasn't until midway through the second that they posed their first threat. They had reached the Chargers' eight on a second down. On third, the quarterback completed a pass into the end zone but one of his own linemen was called for holding. His next pass was intercepted.

The Chargers took over on their own twenty. Mackin completed a beautiful pass for a 42-yard gain. And then, quite simply, he threw again—a bomb right into the end zone. Touchdown.

Midway through the third quarter Mackin led another charge downfield, feeding his backs and grinning (I was sure) as they scrambled past the Cowboy defenders like so many tackling dummies. After making it to the Cowboys' twenty-eight on third down, he rocked back to throw once more. He had a receiver clear near the Dallas ten, but he hesitated a fraction too long. Down Mackin went, grabbed from the left by a safetyman and then flattened by a tackle as well. When the camera started rolling again, the field goal team was on—and missed.

The Cowboys came back and made it fourteen to seven. The game then settled down into typical, cautious Super Bowl play. Only Mackin wasn't in it.

I stopped the projector and reran the play in which he was sacked. The hit hadn't looked that hard but it was conceivable he had twisted an ankle or a knee going down. I'd have to find out.

Shortly into the fourth quarter, the Cowboys threatened to tie it up. But once again they were stopped. A flash-frame and Mackin was back, seemingly favoring his right leg as he moved off the line. But leg or no leg, he engineered a beautiful drive, grinding out yards, mixing plays well, using up the time. A shot of the clock indicated the two minute warning. The Chargers were on the Cowboys' fifteen, and presumably Mackin went over to talk to Sims during the time-out. It was third down and I assumed Sims would want Mackin to hand off down the middle, setting up the field goal attempt on the next down to put the game away.

Mackin took the snap. I saw Chip tear downfield along the right sideline, the linebacker shadowing him, while Peters, the other back, hovered to Mackin's left. Chip appeared open. But Mackin was moving back, still moving back, until he had waited too long. The pocket collapsed and, just as Mackin was throwing, he was blindsided. The ball sailed lazily up in the air and drifted down, right into the waiting arms of a jubilant Cowboy.

"Goddam," I said and then, with a start, realized I had said a few other things, too. I also realized my notepad was empty from the first quarter on, and that the film was flapping noisily behind me.

I stood up to rethread the spool and ran the interception again. Sims could have given him the option of throwing, though it didn't seem to make sense. And why had he kept going back like that? Why hadn't he thrown it away when he saw the pocket collapsing?

Again the film flapped, and I was reaching over to switch off the projector when I realized there was someone else in the room.

I looked up and froze.

Chapter 13

He stood statue-still in the doorway, all six-feet-five of him, splendidly turned out in a navy double-breasted sport coat, white flannel slacks, and Gucci loafers. A commanding presence indeed, with his full head of snow white hair. Except for the stormy gray eyes, he looked just like his pictures. I had no idea how long he had been standing there.

"Forgive my language, Mr. Crittenden."

"Miss Hollis, I don't have enough time to forgive all your sins."

"Oh." The room was so still it was as if it, too, were frightened of this austere figure. Even the film flapping beside me, seemed to do so tentatively. "I'd better switch off the projector," I said meekly.

"DON'T TOUCH IT."

"No, sir."

"JUST SIT DOWN."

"Well, okay, thanks," I said, sinking into the chair.

"The police should be here any minute," he said through clenched teeth.

"The police?" I echoed vaguely.

"Breaking and entering and heaven knows what else."

I stared at him. "You're not serious," I said in disbelief.

"Or illegal trespassing. It matters not to me."

"But that's ridiculous," I protested.

"You've done nothing but make trouble for us all week," he

went on. "And I'm going to put a stop to it."

I began to panic. I could envision the flashing lights and the screeching sirens and an enormous pair of handcuffs. But before I could say anything further, he turned on his heel and marched out the door. Just before slamming it, he said, "I don't see how your father could permit such behavior." Then he was gone.

I sat staring at the door listening to the film beating itself silly. Ridiculously I began to laugh. Maybe Miss Hernandez hadn't been joking about the players' hides after all, I thought, and wondered what he did to players who fumbled. Then it struck me that maybe he had actually locked me in. I grabbed my purse and hurried across the room. The knob turned, the door opened. A voice drifted out of the office next door. A second rumbled.

"Well? What did he say?"

I didn't wait for Miss Hernandez to reply. I took off down the hall and made a beeline for the reception room. Dashed through it, down another dark winding corridor and out to the elevator. I frantically stabbed the button.

"STOP HER!"

I turned and saw the startled look on Miss Hernandez' face as she stood in the doorway beside Crittenden's shaking finger. Then the elevator arrived.

And I departed.

I sat on my bed blowing wobbly smoke rings and wondered if Crittenden could really get me for illegal entry. Probably not. On the other hand, it would lend a nice footnote to the whole affair. I leaned back against the pillows, set the phone on my stomach, and dialed the L.A. office. Eventually Al Larkin, the bureau chief, came on the line. I knew him only through the well-researched, and often wry, memos he sent me. The one on Mackin had been masterful. Among other things, Larkin had reported that Mackin's shirts had to be tailor-made because his right forearm was three inches larger than his left. And that Mackin was tired of people asking him if he wore green contact lenses (he did not).

I told Al I was in San Diego.

"God, you're fast," he said. "I just found out fifteen minutes ago."

"Found out what?"

"That Mackin's got the flu."

"The what?"

"I finally got through to Bill Owens because Happy Harley wasn't returning my calls. Owens said they had been trying to keep it quiet because God forbid the St. Louis Cardinals should find out and perform black magic over Mackin's effigy. But apparently our hero is recovering nicely and should arrive in New Orleans sometime tomorrow."

"Have you checked the airlines?" I said skeptically.

"Christ, no. Should I? I mean what's the big deal?"

"Actually," I went on, "I've called you about something else. I need to pick your brain, or your files. Mackin was injured in the Chargers-Cowboys Super Bowl game. Do you recall what it was?"

"Yeah, but hang on, I've got the file right here." Whoever Larkin was, I mused, I hoped I'd get a chance to meet him. He always sounded like a slightly excited child. "Got it," he said. "Minor ankle sprain. They taped him up and sent him back in. Aren't you getting a little detailed?"

"Trivia question," I said. "What kind of shaving cream does Mackin use?"

"Gillette Foamy."

"Wrong. That's what he advertises. Rapid Shave's in his medicine cabinet along with how many bottles of pills?"

"Uh, two thousand?"

"Two thousand and three. Do you suppose the injury could have accounted for that final interception?"

"To the contrary," said Al excitedly. "It was a gutsy play. You forget the wind factor. I was out there and I remember thinking at the time that White would have trouble with a field goal. And he would have, too."

"So Mackin figured he'd have a better chance scoring on a low pass?"

"Exactly."

"One more question, Al. Is Crittenden really as berserk as he seems?"

"Absolutely. Certifiable, I should think. Why?"

I told him about my run-in that morning.

"Jesus," he said laughing. "If I were you, Lindsie, I'd get out of town. The police down there aren't exactly adverse to accepting a free game ticket or two."

"How about a reporter's bribe?"

"Call me first."

I put the phone back on the table and examined what Al Larkin had told me through a fresh set of smoke rings. I didn't think that what I had was enough to convince Maxwell to hold the story. But maybe it would make him less mulish on Tuesday. I climbed off the king-size bed and went into the bathroom. Grabbed a handful of vitamins and a glass of water. Then I divided my pills into little piles—three oblong vitamin C's, two blood-red B complexes, two B-6's for good measure, an ugly brown iron, the combination A and D, and the nut-flavored chewable E's. When they were all laid out on the bedside table, I placed my call to Maxwell. While I waited for Marianne to put me through, I swallowed the B-6's; they're supposed to make you calm.

"Yes, Lindsie." Maxwell sounded tired, or maybe just resigned.

I went straight for the jugular,"I'd like to try to persuade you to hold the Mackin cover," I came right out and said.

"Impossible."

"They're saying Mackin has the flu."

"I know that," Maxwell said. "Larkin called."

"That's almost as good as saying he checked into a seminary. For starters, he's not home."

"All right, Lindsie. What else?"

"I still can't substantiate this but there's a good possibility Mackin insured a point spread in a Super Bowl game six years ago."

"That's preposterous," said Maxwell automatically.

"Chip Tobias told me that he and Mackin had been approached by a man offering them, quote, gobs of money, unquote, to keep the spread under ten. I later found out that translated into $50,000. Chip said he and Alex took it as a joke. But the Chargers won by seven and five weeks later Mackin deposited $50,000 in a San Francisco bank."

"Pure speculation."

"In a *checking* account, sir. No interest."

"Maybe he didn't want to pay taxes on it," Maxwell reasoned.

"Or maybe he didn't want the IRS looking into it," I pointed out.

"Go on."

"Mackin has a checkbook from that bank but no checks have been torn out of it and there are no entries recorded. But there is the deposit slip. By the way, all of his other accounts are with San Diego banks."

"I won't even ask you how you know this," Maxwell grumbled.

"I just looked at the game film," I went on, "and don't ask me how I did that either. But with a fourteen point lead midway through the third quarter, Mackin went out with a minor ankle sprain. The Cowboys scored and Mackin came back in just in time to throw an interception to end the game."

"And you think he did that on purpose?"

"Can't tell. Al says the wind was blowing in and might have deflected a field goal. There's no way to know, just as there's no way to know about the ankle."

"What else?"

"This is the part I can't compute. Those guys who visited Mackin Sunday night were from Las Vegas, or had recently been there. When I heard about the shift in odds, I thought maybe they had done something to him."

"And now you think he is actively involved?"

"I don't know. If he is I should think he would have shown up in New Orleans on time. Business as usual and all that."

"So it's possible something *has* happened to him," said Maxwell grudgingly. He was obviously thinking of the trouble it would cause him.

"I'm not sure about that either," I admitted. "Apparently he was home for a very brief time. '

Maxwell didn't say anything for a long while. I heard a loud sucking noise. Undoubtedly he had his pipe going. "So you want to hold Mackin a week, is that it?"

The sudden thought of holding Mackin for a week sort of turned me on. I said, "Yes, sir."

"Which would put us in a fine mess," Maxwell said sourly. "If we sub the ballet cover we'll get wiped off the stands."

"Maybe *Time* will hold off, too," I said helpfully.

"Of course they won't," Maxwell said irritably. "They think he's got the flu. I know! So they'll come out with *their* Mackin cover and *Newsweek's* got Redford.

"Oh."

"And what we've got is a whole lot of circumstantial gobbledygook from a reporter who apparently broke into an apartment if not a goddammed bank."

"No," I said quickly. "What's really bothering you is the thought of bringing down a national monument."

"It could cost us a fortune in litigation," he said forbiddingly.

"Lots of people like ballet," I said hopefully.

Suddenly it sounded as if Maxwell had been joined by a woodpecker. Then I realized he must have been tapping his pipe into the ashtray.

"All right," he said abruptly. "I'll give you twenty-four hours. No, twenty-one. If you don't have something more concrete by noon tomorrow, our time, we go to press with Mackin."

"Twenty-one hours?" I said faintly.

"Maybe the son of a bitch is in a hospital."

"Or a seminary." I hung up and swallowed the rest of my pills.

I tried to think through another set of smoke rings. No good. Got up, opened a window, gazed out at the turquoise sky, down at the sparkling sidewalks. I don't know if they put glitter in the cement or what, but somehow San Diego always seemed to sparkle while Boston, even during its three days of summer, always looked like a quick dust job. Still couldn't think. Even downtown the air smelled sweet. Twenty-one hours and not a single lead.

Had to clear my head of fog, my lungs of smoke. I retrieved my shiny white Vega from the hotel garage and steered it onto U.S. 5 North. Off on Garnet Street through Pacific Beach, up to Mackin's gleaming white villa. No answer. Up La Jolla Boulevard and into La Jolla, where the roads were clogged with Cadillacs and the cliffs with mansions. I stopped at a drugstore for a newspaper and eventually found a quiet public beach. Had to think.

But it wasn't happening. My mind kept wandering, along with my eyes, to the two sunbathing teenagers, the frisbee-playing cocker spaniel, the mom making sandcastles with the shrieking little girl. And back to me.

I was twenty-eight and feeling old. "What's happened to you?" Chip had asked, and even on the riverboat there had been all those painful silences. "You're not married," my father had said. Which bothered me because I had been wondering lately if I ever would be. And was beginning to doubt it because the work had to come first.

It probably went back to childhood when I had felt the need to prove myself to my father and three brothers, all of whom would have felt greatly relieved had I been able to toss a football with them. The insecurity I had developed long ago had never gone away. Now Mackin. Football again. Things don't change.

I put on my sunglasses and picked up my newspaper. The lead article on the sports page said Mackin was now due in New Orleans on Sunday. A touch of the flu, he'd be okay. I scanned the rest of the paper and was flipping through the real estate section when my eye caught a splashy half-page ad for Grand Pacifica Estates—"Condomaximums for maximum living." The most luxurious condominiums on the West Coast, it said. And then, at the bottom, "A Presentation of Royce Dion & Associates, Developers."

I lay the paper on my lap and gazed out at the ocean. Follow the money and you end up at a condominium. I thought they had been talking about a Rolls Royce so I had said, "Alex has a Rolls," and he had said, "No, I traded it in on a porch."

Only it hadn't been a Rolls Royce. Just a Royce. "She looks like Royce's gallump, don't you really, Sam?" Because that's where they had watched the games, at Dion's.

I pushed my sunglasses on top of my head and leaned back. The sun felt hot on my face and the sound of the waves was soothing. Occasionally a child's laughter broke through, or the scolding of a bird. After a while, I stood up. And walked slowly back to my car.

"Miss Lipsky?"

"Yes! And you must be Mrs. Hollis. Please sit down, I'm so *glad* you've come."

I was Mrs. Hollis because, as I had told her on the phone, my husband, an attorney in Boston, had suggested I look for investment property while I was visiting friends in San Diego. I had told her this because when I dialed the number printed in the ad, it was she who had answered. Information had no listing for Royce Dion & Associates.

"It's nice of you to see me so soon," I said politely.

"Why I'm delighted you've come. And I think you'll be pleased to see what I have to show you. Let me just get the keys and we'll be off."

While she searched a small cabinet behind her desk, I looked around the office. It was sunny and yellow. Yellow plush carpeting, yellow desk, yellow and white striped shades. Lush green plants shooting out of wicker baskets.

"Must be a pleasant place to work," I observed.

She closed the cabinet door and stood up. She was a tiny, pixie-haired blonde with bright blue eyes and a large toothy smile. I noted her trim green pants suit and yellow print blouse and wondered if she were always color co-ordinated to match the office.

"Some days it's pure delight," she agreed. "Others are ghastly." She rolled her big blue eyes as she hit the word ghastly.

"Why's that?" I supplied.

"People," she sighed. "We get calls from people who say that their very best friends just bought at Grand Pacifica and they want to buy, too, but *puleeze* don't put them in the same building." She laughed. "And, of course, we have interior decorators trooping in and out complaining about this wall and that door. It's mad."

We left the sales office and passed through an enormous mirrored rotunda that was dominated by an enormous chandelier which, she told me, was made of hand-blown glass from Venice. The marble flooring also had been shipped from Italy. It was a nice lobby if you liked looking at yourself.

I said, "I suppose people are pouring a lot of money into the decorating?"

"Oh, my dear," she said, holding the door open for me, "some people are spending as much as they did for the condominium itself." She paused and eyed me speculatively, to see if I might be one of them. "We have one man," she boasted, "who's building a waterfall on his balcony. And there's a big film director from Hollywood who's putting in a screening room. And several people want to turn closets into wine cellars, which means of course, we have to install special thermostats. But come, I'll show you a lovely unit in the middle building, which"—she emphasized—"is my favorite for the view."

There were three crescent-shaped buildings arranged in a semicircle facing the ocean, each five stories high. As we walked, she explained the floor plans.

"Basically the units are alike. They all have a master suite with his and her baths, marble of course, plus dressing rooms, a second bedroom and bath, and a library that could be used as a third bedroom. It has plumbing for a wet bar, but it could also be turned into another bath. The two bedrooms are in a separate wing, but you'll see that. Each floor has only two apartments except for the top, which is a single penthouse. They're double the size of the other units and the ceilings are fifteen feet, but unfortunately, they've all been sold. Come, we'll have to walk up. The elevator isn't working yet."

We had passed through an identical rotunda and she gushed on as we hiked up to the fourth floor . . . for the view, of course. After she had waltzed me through all the rooms and rattled off the amenities, including, "a pull-out tabletop for the maid to eat on," I asked what I figured were the proper questions. And she, eventually, asked me what I thought.

"I'm sure my husband will be *very* interested," I said. And then, just to be cute, "The only problem may be space. We entertain a lot and . . . you say the penthouses are all sold?"

"I'm afraid so. Although—hm—there is one possibility." She brightened. "Yes, I could certainly check. You may be able to buy *both* apartments on this floor and convert them into one."

I casually asked the price.

"Two hundred and twenty-five thousand dollars. For the one, of course."

"Of course."

"And you'd be living right under Grand Pacifica's developer."

"Really?"

"Yes. Mr. Dion. He has fifty percent interest here. And he'll be living right in the building so you won't have to worry about the developers taking off once the condominiums are all sold."

"Is he living here now?" I asked.

"Well, off and on. He's not here at the moment." She paused. "Of course, you have nothing to worry about. He's a lovely man and very much respected. He owns many properties, you know."

"Not, by any chance, in Las Vegas?"

"Why, yes. He owns the Grand Nevada Hotel. Do you know him?"

I said I had heard the name.

It was five o'clock by the time I had driven from Grand Pacifica Estates on the southern tip of Coronado Island back downtown to the Westgate. I stretched out on the bed and tried to figure out what I might say to Royce Dion. The sun, coming in through the windows, was hitting me right between the eyes. I got up and drew the curtains.

I was dreaming that Harley Crittenden and the San Diego police department were pounding on my door, shouting for me to open up, when I heard a distinct click. A key in the lock, the door opening, an unmistakable footstep. I jumped into a sitting position, my heart pounding.

"Just checking."

They do it in the best hotels and I have never understood why they have to burst in like that. Maybe it's because they secretly hate guests and get their kicks by terrorizing us. But this time, after I stopped shaking, I was actually glad she had come. I hadn't meant to fall asleep. And now it was six-fifteen.

I grabbed the phone, called Las Vegas information, and put through a credit card call.

"Good evening. Grand Nevada."

"Mr. Dion's office, please."

"One moment, I'll ring."

For something to do, I pulled a piece of Kleenex from my purse, spit on it, and began cleaning the ashes off the bedside table.

"Mr. Dion's office, may I help you?"

"Mr. Dion, please."

"I'm sorry, he's not in. Who's calling?"

I took a deep breath. "This is Miss Lipsky. From the sales office at Grand Pacifica? We've got a slight problem. I have some men here who say they want to install a, uh, waterfall on Mr. Dion's balcony. Well, I know nothing about *that.* So I thought I'd better check."

"At this hour?" She was skeptical.

"I thought I might still catch him . . ."

"It seems odd for a delivery to made on a Saturday night."

Oh, Christ, I thought. "Special handling," I said quickly.
"Do you know where he can be reached?"

"He can't." She was emphatic.

"Oh?"

"He's out of the country."

"Where?"

"I'll have him phone you when he returns, Miss Lipsky."

"Surely you must have a number," I persisted. "The men are
threatening to leave the whole thing right here on the nice
yellow carpet in the sales office and I can't have *that.*"

"I'm sorry. I have no way to reach him. I'll leave your
message."

Apparently for Mr. Royce Dion, things like waterfalls could
wait. I conceded the loss and hung up. Settled back on the bed.

Out of the country. Could that mean Mexico? It was only
ten, fifteen miles away. I lit a cigarette and poked the match
into the overflowing ashtray. Assume Mexico. I chewed over
the possibilities. He could have flown out of either Las Vegas
or San Diego. He could have driven in through Tijuana. Or,
if he were as wealthy as he sounded, he might even have flown
in his own plane. I decided, for purposes of self-interest, to
assume the latter. For if he had flown in his own plane, he
would have needed to file a flight plan. If I couldn't track him
that way, it would be a major hassle checking the airlines,
trying to con them into giving out information they were not
supposed to.

I dragged the phone book from under the bedside table and
began thumbing through the yellow pages for airports. There
were twelve. I started with the ones printed in the largest type,

my odds of locating him not the kind gamblers put money on.

But then there's something called beginner's luck. On the fifth try, I learned that Royce Dion had indeed filed a flight plan. From Brown Field the evening before. His destination: Hermosillo, Mexico.

**Chapter 14**

At first I thought I was dreaming again. The pounding on the door. The shouts to open up. This time I reacted more slowly. Rolling over, switching on the lamp, squinting at my watch. Nearly midnight.

More pounding. "Miss Hollis?"

"Just a minute," I answered foggily. I found my trench coat, pulled it on over my nightgown, and walked hesitantly to the door. "Who is it?"

"Police."

The door was double-locked, the chain fastened. I slid back the dead bolt and opened the door as far as the chain would allow it. I peeked out. I was expecting to see Harley Crittenden. Instead I saw a man about six feet tall wearing a beige sport coat and brown slacks. Also a third arm dangling from a left shoulder.

"You don't look like police," I said cautiously.

A wallet flipped open. A badge was held up. "We're sorry to disturb you at this hour," said the man in the beige sport coat. "But we do have some questions to ask you."

I pulled the belt tighter around my waist and unhooked the chain. Two men stood in the hallway. "I'm Sergeant Richard Quaid," said the one. "This is Officer Leon." He gestured to the second man, shorter, stocky, with pock-marked skin and a large black mustache. I nodded wearily to both and motioned them inside.

"Please sit down," I said. "I'll be with you in a minute."

I walked into the bathroom and closed the door. Turned on the tap and brushed my teeth. When I went back out I found Quaid sitting in one of the two upholstered chairs by the window. Leon was sitting backwards on the desk chair. My room-service tray from dinner sat congealing behind his back.

I sat down in the chair by Quaid and said nothing. I wondered if they had the red light flashing down in the street—the car doors open for a speedy getaway to the San Diego jail.

"You're a reporter for *Monday* magazine, Miss Hollis?"

That from Quaid, who sat with his legs crossed at the knees, his hands folded in his lap. He had reddish-brown skin and reddish-brown hair and tiny crow's feet bracketing faded blue eyes. They looked slightly bored.

"No," I said. "I'm an associate editor."

"But your job is to report stories for the magazine?"

"Sometimes report, but mainly write. What's your job?"

He smiled genially. "Finding out what you know about Alex Mackin."

"Why?"

"Mr. Crittenden . . ."

"Right. For a dollar fifty you can both find out on Monday. That is, unless Crittenden has right of prior censorship." He probably had. Plain clothesmen yet, one a sergeant. Crittenden went right to the top.

Quaid smiled again. Leon had his arms wrapped around the back of the chair. His eyes seemed to be wrapped around my legs.

"Miss Hollis," said Quaid, "we could bring you down to headquarters for questioning. But that involves all sorts of paper work. We were hoping you would cooperate for just a few minutes and we could avoid all that."

I sighed. "What do you want to know?"

"Why did you visit the Chargers' offices this morning?"

"To look at a game film."

"Why?"

I closed my eyes and rubbed my forehead. I must have just hit deep sleep and my mind was still muddled. I said, "You know why. I'm doing a story on Mackin."

"How long have you been working on this story?" said Quaid.

I got up and walked over to the bedside table for my cigarettes. "About a week or so," I replied, flicking my lighter.

"And what's the gist of your story?"

I sat down and looked at Quaid. His face, like his voice, was impassive. But he was still doing a lousy job.

I yawned. "It's about his supposed intention to retire. What do you think, sergeant? Do you think he'll quit?"

"You're the reporter," he said mildly, "what do you think?"

I loved his technique. Answering a question with a question. I gave him one back. "Do you believe everything Mackin says?"

"What did he say to you?"

"That he is thirty years old, that he's had it too good all his life, and now he thinks God's going to get him."

"I beg your pardon?"

"He thinks he's going to die. Probably soon."

Quaid put his hand in his pocket. "That's interesting," he said, and pulled out a roll of Clorets.

Leon said, "Real nice guy that Mackin. I met him a couple of years ago when he was over at one of the shopping centers autographing his book. They sent a couple of us over to keep things orderly, you know, to keep people from rushing him. He . . . hey! How do you like that? Rushing him. Pretty good, huh?"

I told him it was swell.

"Can you imagine?" Leon went on. "The guy needs protection from girls."

"Women," I said.

"Them, too. Jeez, what a life. Nice guy for it, though. He even gave me a copy of his book. What's it called? *The Quizzical Quarterback?*"

"Quintessential," I said.

"Right. And he autographed it, too. My wife went bananas. Practically slept with the damn thing."

"Did he say why he thought he was going to die?" Quaid interrupted.

Good grief, I thought. "Just what I told you," I said. "What's this got to do with the game film?"

He shrugged. "It doesn't. I just thought that your being a reporter, you would want to pick up on that. May I have one of your cigarettes?"

I knew that trick, too. I passed him the pack, and then, in a masterly stroke I thought, whipped out my lighter and lit it for him. He said, "Where did you interview Mackin?"

"In his apartment."

"When?"

I sighed. "Sunday night."

"And you waited all this time . . . why didn't you get him to show you the film himself? He has all those films, doesn't he?"

"Frankly," I said, "it never occurred to me."

"Didn't it, Miss Hollis?"

"Please call me Lindsie and, no, it did not."

Quaid puffed on the cigarette. "Then why," he said exhaling, "were you in Mackin's apartment last night?"

I felt the cigarette slip through my fingers. I looked at Quaid's still impassive face and knew with a sinking feeling that I had been right all along. The NFL report Doug Finney had seen had been fiddled. There *had* been a fix and Crittenden knew about it. And now he wanted to find out what I knew. Well, I was going to give him an earful.

"All right," I said. "My interview with Mackin was interrupted." I told them about Willy and Sam and how Mackin had said they were bodyguards. I told them I thought I had been drugged which my doctor confirmed. That I went back to Mackin's apartment solely to look in his medicine cabinet because I was considering pressing charges.

Quaid didn't seem particularly impressed, but like a good interviewer he nodded in all the right places. When I finished, he said, "What did Sam and Willy look like?"

I described them. Quaid took notes, or pretended to. "Is there anything else you can recall?"

I told them I had heard Royce Dion's name mentioned and that Mackin had broken a lot of dates that week and I thought it odd that if he went to the mountains he had neglected to take his car.

Quaid snapped his notebook shut and stood up. "We'll look into Willy and Sam for you, Lindsie, and we'll be in touch."

Oh sure, I thought. Fat chance they'd implicate friends of Mackin over such a trivial matter as drugging a reporter.

"As far as Mackin disappearing," he went on, "I think you've let your imagination run away with you."

"Oh, really?" I said. "Then tell me, sergeant. Where *is* Alex Mackin?"

Quaid looked at me in surprise. Then he laughed. "Why, he's at Harley Crittenden's house."

"With the flu."

Quaid shrugged. "It happens to the best of us. Good night, Lindsie."

He took a couple of steps. "Oh. By the way. It'll be up to Alex whether he wants to press charges against you for illegal entry." He smiled. "Good night."

I closed the door after them—and wished I hadn't watered his plants.

The rolling green farmland rose and dipped outside my windows as I sped along Otay Valley Road. It was a nice day for a Sunday drive. I had the windows down, the radio on, and the road to myself. It seemed in no hurry to get anywhere. I was.

After learning that Dion had flown to Hermosillo, I had spent two hours on the phone. Trying to check hotels. But where AT&T ends, the world drops off. I might have done better using a string and two orange juice cans. Anyway, the two hotels I finally reached had no Dion in the house.

And still the road twisted and undulated mile after annoying mile until, just as I was ready to turn back, out jumped a hand-painted sign announcing flying lessons ahead.

I drove in through the gate, down a black-topped road and past a series of former Navy barracks until I found a parking lot that contained more small planes than cars. I left my not-so-white Vega among them and walked toward a low-slung olive green building. A turquoise glass tower rose out of the center of it. Purple mountains loomed darkly in the background under a bright blue sky. It was almost noon. It had taken me that long to drive to San Diego Airport, get a tourist card from a friend of Al Larkin's who worked for the airlines, and then find out that the only way to get to Hermosillo was out of Tijuana on the single Aeromexico flight that flew there each day. It had been booked solid. It was noon, and I had to get back to Maxwell.

Inside the building I found a deserted cafeteria off to the right and a bulletin board straight ahead. Tacked to it were small white cards advertising flying lessons and single-engine craft for sale. Also a large map of North America. I located Hermosillo several inches south of the border and one inch in from the Gulf of California. Then I wandered down a long hall off to the left until I found a door marked Arthur Leen, Fixed Base Operator. The door was open.

A trim man with a brown crewcut was sitting behind a cluttered desk polishing a pair of eyeglasses with a fresh handkerchief.

"Mr. Leen?"

He hurriedly put on his glasses as if he had been caught committing an indiscretion. "Yes?"

"I spoke to you on the phone last night about Mr. Dion. Do you have a moment?"

His eyebrows climbed over the rim of his glasses, pushing his hairline back on his head. He coughed and nodded to a green plastic chair.

I sat down and fiddled with the strap of my purse. "I wonder," I began hesitantly, "if you could tell me who else was aboard."

He tilted his head back and sighted me down the end of his nose. "Now why is that, Miss . . . ?"

"Hollis," I said. "Lindsie Hollis. Well, I think my husband George may have gone with him."

His face reddened. "Oh, I see," he mumbled clearing his throat. "All right, let me check." He shuffled through a stack of papers on his desk, extracted a sheet, and frowned at it. "All it says here is that he had three passengers and his pilot. The names are not given."

"Isn't that . . . I mean, don't you have to keep some kind of record for customs?"

He put the paper on top of the stack and leaned back in his chair. "We're supposed to. But the U.S. government doesn't care so much who goes out as who comes in. Actually, we know Mr. Dion because he's in and out all the time. Flying business folks back and forth to Vegas and sometimes slipping down into Mexico.

"Oh, dear." I hesitated. "You, uh, wouldn't know where he stays in . . . was it Hermosillo? You see my mother's been taken

108

ill and I don't want to leave the kids alone. The babysitter said she could only stay until dinner."

Leen considered. "Seems to me he's got a little place down there where he takes folks fishing but I wouldn't know how you could reach him."

"In Hermosillo?"

"No. But the Gulf's only about sixty miles due west." He pinched his nose and pushed his glasses up.

I sighed. "I wish I knew what to do. Do you suppose the airport in Hermosillo would have a record of who was aboard?"

"Customs man sure would."

"Perhaps I could call . . ."

Arthur Leen cut me off with a sharp laugh. "You ever tried calling Mexico?" he said bitterly. "You'd be on the phone a week."

"Oh." I hesitated. "Mr. Leen, what would you suggest?"

He looked at me irritably. He obviously didn't want any part of my domestic problems. He said, "I'd like to help you but . . ."

I opened my purse and found my cigarettes. If he didn't get the hint that I was here to stay I could always bring out a piece of Kleenex. He got the hint. "All right, Mrs. Hollis. There is a possibility. We have a guy getting ready to fly down there now to deliver some fabric to a lady. Maybe he could check for you. But don't tell him I said to. You'll have to ask him yourself."

"Where do I find him?"

"He's out on the tarmac right now, fueling up. Redheaded guy, kind of lanky. Goes by the name of Skip."

I found Skip crouching beside the wheel of a toy-sized single-engine plane. "Excuse me," I said.

Slowly he looked up. "Yes, ma'am?"

"I understand you're going to Hermosillo."

"Yes, ma'am. Here, could you hold this for a minute?" He

handed me a filthy rag and dug into the pocket of his overalls for a metal tool. He began diddling with the wheel.

"I was wondering if you could do me a small favor," I said and told him what I wanted. He kept right on diddling. Eventually he stood up and wiped his hands on his overalls.

"Let me get this straight," he said. "You want me to fly you down and back?"

"As long as you're going anyway."

He shook his head. "I don't take passengers." He began peeling off the overalls.

I considered the top of his red head as he bent over. I said, "How much money do you want?"

He brought his eyes up to mine, counting dollars as he went. "Hundred bucks."

"Seventy-five," I said handing him the rag. "I get a discount for maintenance."

12:45. Forty-five minutes past deadline. Through the window I could see Skip loading a brown paper parcel into the plane.

"Sir? This is Lindsie."

"Where are you?" Maxwell demanded.

"Where . . . why San Diego. Look, I've got a lead but I'll need another couple of hours."

"I see," Maxwell said slowly. "Hm . . . no. Can't wait. We'll go with ballet."

I sighed with relief.

"And I want you to fly to New Orleans right away. How soon can you get a flight?"

That jolted me. "I don't know . . . why?"

"Mackin's arriving today. I want you to get to him."

"Yes, but . . ."

"Not buts, Lindsie." He was emphatic. "And call me the minute you arrive. I'll be at home."

I said okay and walked out to the plane. If they were holding the Mackin cover, there was no reason to rush to New Orleans. I could still try to find Dion and catch a flight later that night. I climbed into the plane and watched Skip fiddle with all those dials that somehow did something to get us off the ground.

Then I watched the airplane's shadow poke along the desert floor. And thought about that final interception.

I awoke to find a tipsy Hermosillo lurching drunkenly under our wings. Skip set the plane down smoothly just as the runway righted itself and we rolled up to the miniature terminal, parking next to an Aeromexico DC9.

I located Senor Ortega, the customs man, standing damply behind a table stamping passports. He was a short, square man with a smooth black mustache. A commanding figure in every respect, I soon learned, except English. When it was my turn, I dug down deep and dredged up some freshman Spanish 101.

Yes, he knew Senor Dion. Yes, his plane was here. Why? Who was I?

I went through my lost husband routine because it seemed the most plausible reason to be asking about Dion.

Ortega nodded and eventually led me into a small office. A dusty window looked out over the tarmac. As he searched a filing cabinet, I watched people boarding the DC9. In time, he yanked a folder from the drawer, removed a single sheet of paper, and handed it to me. It was written in Spanish but the words Beechcraft Baron came through and I was able to make out the "purpose of the visit"—pleasure. Under the names of passengers were four: Royce Dion, William Henderson, Jake Morris, and a Tom Byers. The pilot was George Lucas.

Were any of those men my husband? No, but maybe they might know where my husband was. Did Ortega know where I could find them?

He shrugged his square shoulders and yawned.

All the passengers had boarded when I walked back into the terminal. It wasn't the kind of airport you'd want to get hung up in. Flanking either side of the main entrance were what looked like hotdog stands. Stretched across each counter and secured by vertical poles were signs. One said Avis. The other, Hertz. Beyond the Avis stand, a pretty Mexican girl was tidying up a cluttered gift counter. Across from the gift stand stood the airport restaurant, a few scattered tables set off from the rest of the lounge by low boxes filled with tropical plants.

The Hertz counter was unattended, so I approached a dreamy-eyed teenager who was lounging under the Avis sign.

I smiled and asked if he were Senor Avis.

A pair of enormous black eyes blinked back to the present. "Oh, no senorita! I am Jaime." And then seeing my wink he broke into a broad grin.

"You speak English, Jaime?"

"Oh, yes," he boasted. "You want wheels?"

I laughed. "Maybe. But first I was wondering if you were working last night."

He wrinkled his nose. "Jaime always work."

"Did you rent a car to some norteamericanos who came in a private plane?"

He started to nod, then stopped. "I not so sure," he said evasively.

I put two dollar bills on the counter. The money disappeared into his pocket, and Jaime disappeared behind the counter. A moment later he bobbed back up clutching a stack of Avis rental forms. Painstakingly, he studied each of the first three sheets, eventually decided on the fourth and, looking furtively around him, slid it across the counter to me.

The Avis form reported that a Volkswagen Thing had been rented to Royce Dion at 6:57 P.M the night before. I looked at the boy and smiled.

"Did the man say where he was going, Jamie?"

The look of uncertainty returned. I dug out two more dollar bills. His eager hand streaked across the counter and snatched the money.

"He ask how far to Bahia Kino."

"Where's that?"

Jaime turned and pointed out the door. "You just get on that road and go to the right."

"How far is it?"

"Oh, maybe eighty kilometers. One hour."

I wondered why Dion, who supposedly came here often, had made a point of asking directions. Without finding an answer, I slid my Avis credit card across the counter and ordered up one ancient, dusty, dark blue Renault.

The two-lane highway ran straight as an arrow across the brown desert sand as if racing the sun to the distant Gulf waters. Occasionally a strong gust of wind threw up a curtain of dust across the road and I had to brake hard and crawl blindly through it. The glimmering turquoise water at last came into view and the road took a sharp right to avoid plunging into it. For a mile or so, the road paralleled the water before being pushed farther to the left by a widening wedge of sand. A sign informed me I was entering Bahia Kino, a sprawling metropolis that lasted for the blink of an eye.

To my right, several tiers of garishly painted vacation homes clung to a steep hill. Gradually, the hill leveled off and wound down into Kino's business district: two motels and a combination general store-restaurant.

I parked the creaky Renault along the tree-lined main street and walked back to the store. A middle-aged Mexican in a soiled blue shirt was leaning over a dusty glass-topped counter filled with aspirin, Bandaids, pipe tobacco, and candy bars. To his right, a couple of teenagers sipped Cokes and fed coins into a small juke box attached to their table. The man behind the counter greeted his third customer with a vivid display of utter boredom.

"Buenos, senor."

He blinked.

"Habla Inglés?"

No response.

I tried a smile. "Conoce Senor Royce Dion?"

He scratched his arm pit.

Well, then, had he seen any gringos lately?

He nodded, barely.

Did he know who they were?

He yawned. Some boys from the school Outward Bound had dropped in to pick up supplies.

What did they look like?

He shrugged.

Behind him were shelves filled with loaves of bread, boxes of cereal and laundry detergent, tins of soup and vegetables, packages of cookies, and sacks of sugar and flour. An ancient refrigerator streaked yellow with dirt stood on its last legs in the corner. A phone clung to the wall.

Was there another supermercado in town, I asked, politely upgrading his establishment.

An imperceptible shake of the head.

I noticed the price stamped on a can of peas. Twice what I paid in Boston.

Where do people buy food?

The food, he mumbled, comes from the sea. And, I added to myself, the tourists get ripped off.

I ordered a cup of coffee and sat down in one of the booths along the windows facing the street. It was quarter to five by my watch and I hadn't much time until I would have to start back. Skip had told me he'd be leaving for San Diego around seven-thirty. And I still had to get to New Orleans.

Just as I was swallowing the last drop of coffee, a young man in faded jeans walked through the door. Though he spoke fluent Spanish to the Mexican, his accent was clearly American. He was asking for mail. The Mexican opened a drawer under the cash register and started sorting through a stack of letters. As he handed the envelopes over, I stepped up to the American.

I said hi.

He looked at me in surprise and said hi back. He was tall and lean and quite tan. A cowboy hat tilted over his right ear. I glanced swiftly at the top letter in his hand and saw the words Outward Bound underlined in blue ink. As a reporter, I long ago perfected the art of reading upside down.

"I'm supposed to meet some Americans here," I said. "Do you by any chance know Royce Dion?"

"Don't believe I do," he drawled.

"He's here with three other Americans. Maybe you've seen them."

"No, I sure haven't. Course this is the first time I've been to town in three days. We've got a group of Coors executives traipsing around on a survival hike. But no one by that name."

"Are there any other stores or restaurants where they might have gone?"

He looked at me with amused eyes. "Not in Kino. There are some places farther down the coast though. Only one restaurant here, but if your friends aren't familiar with the town, I doubt they'd know about it."

"Is it far?"

"Not so far as difficult to find. But if you want to go, I'll point the way. I have to drive past there anyway."

I said I'd be right along and asked the Mexican if he would

accept an American quarter. He said he would not, but he would take two.

The Outward Bound man was waiting for me on the sidewalk. I told him my car was parked just down the street.

"Follow me then," he said, jumping into a battered light blue pick-up truck.

The sun was almost gone and the air had grown chill. I rolled up my window and followed his taillights down the main street. Downtown Kino disappeared in my rearview mirror and all that remained of civilization were a few shacks scattered near the water. The apron of sand grew wider until the water disappeared from sight. We must have gone about a mile and a half when the truck took an abrupt left and began bulldozing bumpily through low brush and scrub cactus. I followed cautiously, more in the interests of preserving my doddering Renault than in preserving the ecology. Suddenly the truck plunged to a stop. I rumbled up beside it, leaned across the seat and rolled down my window.

"You're kidding," I said.

"I warned you," he said.

"Okay, but aside from cactus, what else is on the menu?"

He sighted along his arm. "See that place there?"

"That *shack?*"

"House," he corrected. "That's it. Just go in and tell them Stretch sent you. Fish is marvelous." And with that, he rolled up his window and thundered off.

I sat there in the growing darkness listening to the fading crunch of his tires and the moaning of the wind, tempted to chase after him and get back to Hermosillo. But the house was just ahead and I figured another few minutes wouldn't hurt. My reluctant Renault obviously thought it would.

I pulled up beside the whitewashed wooden house and turned off the engine. Attached to the rear of the building was a cluttered tool shed. Near it, two metal poles supported a clothes line that held a couple of billowing sheets. I could hear the gentle lapping of waves from somewhere up ahead.

I walked up three sagging steps and pulled open a screen door. A single bulb dangled from the ceiling illuminating an enclosed porch. There were five or six small square tables, each covered with a soiled oilcloth. Through a door at the rear, I could see a very large refrigerator and a very small girl.

She walked shyly toward me, a child of maybe eight, with great black eyes and long stringy hair. She wore a little white smock that was smudged with dirt.

Unexpectedly, she reached for my hand and led me to one of the tables. I hadn't intended to stay for dinner but I felt suddenly guilty about simply asking for information and leaving my little waitress empty-handed. She smiled happily as I sat down and proudly spread a paper napkin on my lap. She disappeared into the kitchen.

Presently I could hear the crackle of hot oil and I could see an elderly man bent over the stove. The little girl stood importantly at his side. About fifteen minutes elapsed before she returned to my table and timidly nudged a plate in front of me.

"Le gusta tortillas?" she lisped.

"Si. Muchas gracias."

Covering the entire paper plate was an enormous fish, I didn't know what kind. Also several thin leaves of lettuce and a slice of tomato. A moment later the little girl added a stack of warm tortillas to my plate.

Hesitantly, I bit into a tiny piece of fish and found it delicious. I folded up a tortilla and began gobbling up the meal, suddenly realizing how hungry I was. The little girl came back and asked if I would like *cafe*. I said yes.

And then as she was pouring my coffee I felt my insides knot up. And I must have stared at her wide-eyed, because she began backing off with her coffee pot, bumping into a table and fleeing for the kitchen. I suddenly knew why Maxwell had readily subbed the ballet cover and told me to rush to New Orleans. Why two plainclothes officers had come to my hotel room at midnight. Not to question me about seeing the game film or even illegally entering Mackin's apartment. They couldn't have known about the apartment because the rental lady wasn't the type to call them. No, they had come to her. And she had mentioned it. And then they had called Maxwell. And Maxwell had ordered me to New Orleans, not to interview Mackin. Because Mackin wouldn't be there, but to make sure I got the hell out of San Diego. Maxwell knew and the police knew and Crittenden knew. But nobody had told me. And I had walked right into the target area.

I jumped.

But it was only a small woman carrying a baby and a bag of groceries, trailed by three other children. She glanced at me curiously before disappearing into the kitchen. When she came out seconds later carrying a sponge, I called to her, tried to be calm, complimented her on the meal, and asked how much I owed.

"Quatro pesos, por favor," she replied hesitantly.

"Quatro?" I said incredulously. Sixteen cents? She nodded sheepishly. I told her I had only American money and would she please accept a dollar.

She said to wait a moment. She would get change. I hurried outdoors before she could return.

It was pitch black by then and a million stars shone brightly from another world. But I didn't stop to admire them. I wanted only to beat it back to Hermosillo, get on Skip's plane and get the hell out of there.

My car had been joined by a decomposing flatbed truck and a jeep. But it wasn't until I had my hand on the door

that I realized there should have been only one other vehi-
cle, the woman's. By then it was too late. The door opened
and the interior light went on. Behind the wheel, grinning,
sat Willy.

Pointing a gun.

Chapter 15

He slid out of the driver's seat and rose phantomlike before me, the car light gouging eerie hollows in his cheeks. He had no eyes, just two black spaces. The wind blew his hair straight up.

Slowly, I began moving backward, out of the patch of light and into the darkness. I hit the side of the house.

He didn't speak. Just kept coming, his lips curved in a strange smile, until all that stretched between us was the short barrel of the gun.

Time passed. I could hear each sound distinctly. The slapping of the waves, the sheets flapping on the clothes line, the muffled voices from within the house. I could feel the prickles on my skin and my hair blowing across my face. I opened my mouth to speak. And then his arm came up. My head crashed against the side of the house and what had begun as a scream, expired into a sick moan. Behind my shut eyes the night turned to fire.

. . . I could hear him breathing. Could feel the rough material of a sleeve on my face. As I squeezed open my eyes, he grabbed my raised arm and jerked it down, spun me around and twisted it behind my back.

"Don't scream," he enunciated, jacking my arm up even higher.

My heart was pounding and underneath my clothes, I was sweating. Then he did something to my elbow and I nearly cried out.

"I won't. Please—"

The tension on my arm lessened. I straightened slowly. "Please . . . let go. I won't run."

He grunted. And jerked my arm straight down.

"Thank you," I said and stepped back. I went for his instep. Heard the scream and broke loose as he staggered back. I turned and took off for the car. The door was still open . . . ten feet at most. Suddenly my leg locked and I was hitting the sand. I tried to kick loose and then came the soft whoosh. My head exploded into a thousand fragments.

The man in front of me was speaking quick staccato Spanish. But I couldn't grasp what he was trying to tell me.

I drifted off again, wishing the air turbulence would subside and the man would be quiet. He was giving me a vicious headache. When I surfaced again it was after we had hit a deep air pocket. I was nauseous.

Slowly I opened my eyes and through a tangle of hair winced at the bright red and green lights. I tried to sweep the hair out of my face but my hands wouldn't move. I looked down at them. They lay curled in my lap. Tightly bound by a thick brown rope.

I stared at the dashboard and then up at the windshield. All I could see were two bouncing beams of light.

"Won't be much longer," said Willy eagerly.

I sank back in my seat and wondered—till what?

"Where are we?" I asked dully.

It was pitch black outside. Through the scratched and dusty windshield the headlights poked a path through thick Texas-sized brush that towered high above the jeep. The road, if there was one, seemed to consist of two deep ruts from which the civil engineers had neglected to remove the rocks. We weren't in a plane after all; we were on a rollercoaster.

I dragged my thoughts indoors and listened to them squabble

over which part of my anatomy was in worse shape. The debate didn't rage long.

"I'm going to throw up," I said.

No response. I turned and studied his profile. His head nearly touched the roof. He was wearing a look of intent concentration, as he sat hunched over the steering wheel, which was in his lap, peering out through the grimy windshield. I had no idea what kind of picture he was getting; it looked like it had a lot of interference.

My attention leaped from my queasy stomach to my aching head. "Could you please turn the radio off?" I groaned.

A hand the size of a sheepdog's paw lifted off the steering wheel, groped at the dash, and swallowed the dial. The neon numbers faded and the staccato voice drifted away. But not the pounding in my head, and once again as we careened and crashed on, I tasted fish in my throat.

"Talk to me," I moaned, hoping to get my mind off my impending emergency.

"I'm going to kill you," he said, presenting me with another.

My stomach turned over. "Whatever for?" I said inanely.

Willy ran his hand along my thigh, sending shivers down my spine. "So you can't identify us, sweetheart."

We hit another bump and my head hit the roof. I sank deeper into my seat and shut my eyes. "Are you going to kill Mackin, too?"

"Are you crazy?" he demanded. "And have every pig in the country after us? No way."

He was right, I thought grudgingly. Return Mackin safely and eventually the police would give up the search. Kill Mackin and they never would. Kill me and they'd look for awhile. It didn't seem fair just because I wasn't born with my shoulder sockets funny. I sighed. "How did you find me?"

"Mr. Dion has friends," Willy boasted. We leap-frogged another sixty feet. I took a deep breath and swallowed back the bile and wondered who. The airport manager at Brown Field? Skip? Senor Ortega? The Avis boy? The Mexican in the grocery store? The Outward Bound guy? The family that served me dinner? The list was depressingly long. I considered them all and decided the only sure friend Dion had was me. I began working at the ropes.

"How much is the ransom?" I said after a while.

Willy giggled. "One million two hundred thou, darling."

"Jesus," I moaned, "will you watch where you're going?" I didn't like the sound my head had made hitting the metal crossbar. I scrunched down until I was sitting on my tailbone. "When did you phone Crittenden?"

"Yesterday," he said cheerfully.

I thought about that for a while. The brush had grown so dense that it was scraping against the windows. It seemed impossible that this could be leading anywhere. I said, "You've had him since Monday. What took you so long?"

Willy shrugged. "Ask Mackin."

I gave up on the ropes. My hands were already numb. "And if Crittenden doesn't pay up?" I said faintly.

"Then he'll have to find a new quarterback."

That didn't make a whole lot of sense because they'd have the police on them again. It had to be more complicated than that. On the other hand, a kidnapper who boldly flies his own plane into Mexico and then rents a car can't be all that bright. I didn't like that thought at all.

Abruptly the jouncing subsided and the thick brush gave way to a small clearing. Through it I could see a dim light and gradually the dark shape of a cabin. The jeep slammed to a halt, Willy switched off the engine, and dragged me inside.

How they had found this hovel, I could not imagine. It had probably been built and subsisted in by Indians. The walls were of logs and mud; the floor of dirt. Smoke drifted from a blackened fireplace, and everywhere, the stench of fish and cooking oil.

They were playing cards. Sitting by lantern light at a rickety wooden table were Mackin, Sam, and a slightly built, fair-haired man with wire-rim glasses. He wore a pair of chino pants and a heavy red plaid jacket. And he looked furious.

"What is this?" he demanded.

"She's the one we were telling you about, Mr. Dion," said Willy gleefully. "I found her in Kino. She's a reporter." Triumphantly he held up my purse. "I looked through her wallet."

Dion's eyes lit on me. "A reporter for who?"

"Whom," I said.

"What?"

"*Monday* magazine," Willy put in.

"Well how the hell did she get here?"

Four pairs of eyes demanded an answer.

"Willy drove me," I volunteered.

Dion put down his cards and stood up, took several seething steps toward me. Peered at me over the top of his glasses. "Who sent you here, Miss . . . ?"

"Hollis," Willy chimed in.

"Divine inspiration," I added. Cards and beer and only Mackin's feet were tied.

Dion's mouth tightened. "Do you play poker, Miss Hollis?"

The question confused me. Were they that desperate for a fifth? I decided not to answer.

"One thing a poker player learns," Dion said, "is that you can get away with bluffing once in a while. Actually the odds are one hand in five. The other four you'd better be holding the cards. And you, Miss Hollis, don't even hold a busted flush."

I was still trying to get a response out of Mackin. I said, " How about a busted head?"

124

Mackin didn't even blink. Sam swore. Dion looked at me as if I'd just beaten the house.

"How did you find us?" he shouted.

I said nothing.

Willy grabbed my arm. "I'll find out," he said with rising delight.

"Well?" Dion demanded.

"I guess I was just lucky."

Dion stepped forward and slapped my face. That put me somewhere in the vicinity of Willy's middle. I didn't like that but he did. He brought his arm around my waist and squeezed. The air went out of my lungs with a sickening whoosh.

"Tell us," said Dion, flexing his hand.

"The police," I gasped. "I . . . heard them . . . talking."

"Impossible," said Dion.

"She's lying," screeched Willy, tightening his hold.

Sam stood up and came over. "The police couldn't know," he said. "They couldn't know it was Dion."

"Then how did she find out?" Dion challenged.

Sam shrugged. "Just a little too clever for her own good." That, I thought sourly, was it to a tee.

"Maybe," said Sam, narrowing his eyes, "she's been on to us all along. Miss Hollis may know more than we think."

"Don't be silly," said Mackin from across the room.

Sam, Willy, and Dion all turned to him.

"She's just a dumb little reporter," Mackin said disgustedly. "Hell, the only reason she works there is because her father is the head coach for the Bears."

I wondered how he knew that. And then a ray of light began to dawn. And I saw how he had tried to use me to get out of his jam. Now, too late, he was trying to get me out of mine.

"Is he important?" Dion asked.

"Jason Hollis?" said Mackin. "Hell yes."

"We'll have to kill her anyway," Dion declared.

"Now?" said Willy excitedly.

Dion considered me with the practiced eye of a buyer at a cattle auction. "No," he said at last. "We'll do it another way. We'll put her on the plane and arrange for a crash." He smiled wickedly. "That way we'll kill two birds with one stone, so to speak."

"Brilliant," declared Sam. The two laughed.

"Tie her up," Dion said and walked back to the table.

Willy dragged me to the farthest corner of the shack and pushed me roughly to the floor. I landed on my behind and stayed that way. A mistake. He swooped down beside me, placed one enormous hand on my breast and pushed me onto my back. I didn't know what else he had in his twisted little mind but I wasn't about to find out. I brought my knees up and kicked him squarely in the chest. With two-inch heels. He didn't even wince. Rather, a film came over his eyes and he grinned at me . . . slowly and lewdly. Someone began shuffling cards.

I stared at him in icy disbelief. Brought my eyes down and began to panic. The face moving forward . . . the hand on the zipper. The scraping of a chair.

"For God's sake, Willy."

Slowly I looked away from his shining eyes and up into a pair of cold black ones.

"Just tie her feet. You can do what you like tomorrow."

"What difference does it make, huh, Sam?" His eyes were still on me, his hand did not budge from his zipper. I felt my skin crawl.

Sam flicked me a disinterested glance. "Probably none. But tie her up anyway." He went back to his game.

Expressionlessly, Willy reached for a piece of rope and tied my ankles together. Then he smiled slowly, leaned over and

kissed me squarely on the mouth for what seemed an eternity.
I wanted to vomit.

"Jesus, Sam, you sure picked a turkey," said Dion in disgust.

"Let him get it out of his system." A pause. "It's your deal.
Willy?"

At last he stood up, and with a final triumphant look over
his shoulder, Willy joined the others at the table.

Alex Mackin never said a word.

They were moving about at daybreak, rolling up sleeping
bags and stuffing pots and tins of food into a large dufflebag. I
heard them shuffling and clanking about, as I lay shivering on
the hard, damp ground, but I did not look at their faces. Gray
light filtered in through two small windows and made everything look colder and bleaker than the night before. I had heard
them then, too. Breathing, and in one case snoring, and over my
shoulder Mackin had seemed to be fidgeting. I'd wondered
about him all night and into Monday's dreary dawn. I hadn't
slept a wink.

Eventually I jerked myself up into a sitting position. That
produced a new ache and the instant arrival of Willy, Sam, and
Dion.

"I have to go to the bathroom," I said.

They just stared at me.

I looked down at my hands, white blobs of bloated flesh
without a trace of feeling in them, and hoped they would let me.

"Take her out back," Dion snapped.

To my relief, it was Sam who crouched down and began
untying my feet. Willy's big brown boots clumped disappoint-
edly away. I looked at the top of Sam's bald head with the large
ears sticking out and knew then where I'd seen that head before.
Another small piece dropped into place. Then suddenly the
pain surged through my fingers, along with the blood, and I

pressed my hands against my legs in agony. My arm was jerked and I was yanked to my feet.

Outside the air was cold and damp and fresh, the sky colorless and clear. We walked round the back and to the edge of the small clearing. I was allowed to proceed fifteen, twenty feet into the brush, then ordered to stop "right there."

Under the direct gaze of those cold black eyes I turned and began fumbling with my belt. There was nowhere to run to, I thought wearily, and besides, I was in no shape to run anyway. Awkwardly I squatted down into the prickly brush and wondered if anybody would find us.

Back in the cabin, Mackin was slumped against the stone fireplace, staring gloomily at his hands. They had been tied, and he seemed unsure what to do with them. For once he didn't look so gorgeous. His face was streaked with dirt, overgrown with beard, his navy windbreaker lay open revealing a filthy blue work shirt. Even his green eyes had lost their brightness, I noticed, as he watched Sam tie my hands and push me to the ground. Mackin's gaze returned to his lap.

Presently we were loaded into the Volkswagen Thing, Willy at the wheel, Mackin beside him, me sandwiched between the others in back. We began bulldozing back the way we had come the night before.

For hours we drove. Through the brush, out of the brush, onto a flat sandy road. To the left, the Gulf of California caught brilliant sunbeams and relayed them back to heaven. And still we drove mile after mile boring mile, nobody talking, until at last the scrub outside Dion's window thinned out giving way to desert as far as the eye could see. In the distance, a forlorn group of mountains jutted out of nowhere, haphazardly set down for want of a better place, and forgotten.

"Pico Johnson," said Dion. "The tallest one, Willy. That's where we're going."

Another hour. And never once did Alexander Mackin turn around. The little jeep had become an oven. I was sweating under all my clothes, the wool blazer, V-neck sweater, shirt. And still we kept driving, hitting potholes, bouncing into each other, until eventually we began veering off to the right and into a new growth of scrub and small cactuses.

"Hold it," said Dion. "We'll have to hike from here. Later you can hide the car in the brush."

I thought that was pretty funny and had sudden visions of pounding hoofs, only Lawrence of Arabia was dead and John Wayne was too old. But soon it wasn't funny anymore because hiking to the base of Pico Johnson was damn hard work. It didn't help that I, like Mackin, was forced to carry a sleeping bag. With my hands tied, I had to clutch it to my chest, and as it kept slipping, I had to stop repeatedly to hoist it up again. Dion, who carried the third sleeping bag on his shoulder and the duffle in his hand, kept pace with Mackin up ahead. Behind me, Willy and Sam trudged along under the weight of two large water cans each.

We were all sweating hard by the time we arrived at Pico Johnson. Dion threw down his gear, tilted his head back, and studied the mountain. I am no mountain expert, but it looked to be four, maybe five thousand feet high, judging from what I ski on in Vermont. I wished I were there.

"Stay here," said Dion abruptly. He started to walk up a slight incline to the right and continued walking with his narrow back to us. He climbed steadily, diminishing in size as he went, until at last, he disappeared round a bend.

"What's he doing?" said Willy, squinting.

Sam shrugged. "Go take care of the jeep."

Willy lumbered off and Mackin sat down on the duffle bag. "I'm thirsty," he complained.

Sam ignored him and went to sit in the shade. I sat down at

Mackin's feet and leaned against the duffle. Though I was partially in the shade, the heat from the sand rose up and baked my face. It was peacefully quiet. I closed my eyes and waited for Mackin to say something. He shouldn't have been so aloof toward me. I knew they had him in a bind. But what I didn't know was if the kidnapping had been his idea as a way out— or theirs. They just wanted money. And he just wanted them off his back. But would he go this far?

"I'm thirsty," he said again. And Sam ignored him again. And I said, "At least when you're out there insuring point spreads, there's plenty of Gatorade."

Mackin looked at me sharply. "Jesus, Lindsie . . ."

"What?" said Sam.

"Nothing," said Mackin.

"Oh well," I sighed, "I don't suppose anybody will ever be able to prove anything."

"Except you."

"Mm." I closed my eyes again and waited.

With a gravelly thud, Dion returned. "If we go up just a short distance," he said cheerfully, "we'll have better cover. Ah, there's Willy. Ready?"

First Sam and Willy had to lug the gear up, then us. Mackin and I were untied and retied to Willy and Sam. Though the incline was gentle, the mountain proved to be little more than a rubble heap; we kept slipping and sliding on the loose scree. Dion, small and lithe, seemed amused at everybody's clumsy progress.

Eventually we reached a small flat to Dion's liking and, ensemble, collapsed on the ground. Again we were untied and retied. Dion looked at his watch.

"Quarter to three," he announced. "I'd better get going."

"Wait a minute," said Sam. "I want to get this straight." He dug a wrinkled handkerchief from his pocket and wearily mopped the top of his head. I hoped he'd have a nice sunburn.

"Pickup tonight at ten," said Dion. "We fly down tomorrow morning, land in Hermosillo, and on our way back, we'll swing down here and pick you up."

Clever, I thought. The extra few minutes it took to sidetrack to Kino would never be noticed by the flight controllers in San Diego.

" . . . noon. Look for me about then. Willy will drive the jeep back to Hermosillo and catch a flight from there."

It sounded to me like Willy might catch a double-cross.

"Uh, chief," he said, "what if something goes wrong?"

"Give me twenty-four hours leeway. If I'm not here by noon Wednesday, you're on your own."

It sounded like they were all going to be double-crossed.

"What do we do with them?" asked Sam.

"Them?" echoed Mackin. "What do you mean *them?*"

Dion gave him a chilly smile. "Change of plans, my friend. I don't know if she just fell into Hermosillo or what. But if it's a trap, I want to keep my leverage. You stay."

"But that's insane," Mackin shouted. "There's no way Crittenden will hand over the money without me."

"Right," said Dion. "You'll write down a play."

"A what?"

"Write down the running play you called that set up your first touchdown last week."

"For chrissake," exploded Mackin. "What the hell will that prove?"

"Then," Dion went on, "write out the date, Monday, January seventh, and the time, three o'clock, all in longhand. Now."

After a bit of confusion they settled on a paper towel from the duffle and with much grumbling Mackin scribbled out the play. "I'm telling you," he said furiously, "Crittenden will never pay up for a lousy scrap of paper."

"We'll just have to chance it, won't we?" said Dion.

"Goddam," said Mackin, "you promised nothing was going to happen to me. And now you're going to leave me with this lunatic?"

"Now just a minute . . ." began Willy heatedly.

"Let's not talk about promises," Dion cut in. "You had your chance, Mackin. Now you're stuck with mine. And I'd say the odds are fifty-fifty."

"With or without points?" I piped up.

Dion opened his mouth to speak but was interrupted by the soft drone of an engine wafting through the desert heat. We all looked heavenward. A speck of silver flashed in the distance back the way we had come. The speck grew into a plane as the drone became a roar.

"Got to go," said Dion hurriedly. He picked up his red plaid jacket and trotted off. Suddenly, he turned and looked back. He lifted his arm and flashed us the V sign. Then he disappeared around the bend.

The twin-engine Beechcraft Baron landed down to our left and taxied out of sight in front of Pico Johnson. Some time later, it took off, circled overhead, and drifted lazily out over the water. We watched in silence as it grew smaller, a tiny flashing diamond in a vast blue horizon. Finally it disappeared altogether.

"Now I'm going to kill you," Willy said.

And began walking toward me.

Chapter 16

The rocks crunched under his boots. To me, it was the screech of fingernails across a blackboard, and under the hot sun I shivered.

Crunch.

The boots planted themselves firmly two feet from where I sat huddled on the ground. Slowly, I brought my eyes up, my brain, perversely, registering every detail. The mud-caked jeans, the black leather belt, gray T-shirt with perspiration stains under the arms, the arms themselves folded defiantly across his weightlifter's chest. He was glaring down at me with bright hostile eyes. Stringy blond hair fell damply across his forehead.

"Kill you," he said as if in a trance.

"Even," I said desperately, "if it means getting killed yourself?"

He spat. A glob of saliva spattered on the ground at my toe and glistened in the sun. I was sitting with my knees up, my arms hugging them. My clenched hands felt like ice. I tried to remember what I had read about psychopaths, but the information lay tangled somewhere in my head. All that registered was the hungry face above me.

"The police are looking for you," I tried again. "Sergeant Quaid in San Diego. I gave him a description of you. And Sam. He knows you're in Kino."

"No cop's gonna blow me away," Willy sneered. His arms

133

dropped to his sides. He seemed to be balancing on his toes. I was saying the wrong thing. I felt perspiration running down my face.

"Dion won't want you to," I said ridiculously. "You'll get him in trouble for murder. He'll have to kill you. To protect himself."

Willy didn't like that either. Suddenly, he lunged at me, twisting me so that he was behind me. My hair was yanked, my head jerked back. A hand clawed at my neck. I squirmed, threw my arms up instinctively to my throat, but they were tied at the wrists and useless. His fingers dug into my throat and a thousand needles of pain shot through my head as he continued yanking my hair. He had his knee in my back and was twisting my head to the left. I began to gasp for air and I could hear a horrible crunching in my neck, then . . . not even that. Only the pure joyous sound of laughter.

And in my mind the words, "Oh, God . . ." Everything went black.

Somewhere far away, above the roaring in my ears, came the sounds of thumping, scuffling, grunting. And then I tumbled backward onto the ground, felt the dust blow across my face, heard the wheezing in my lungs. As the blackness faded I could see a jumble of arms and legs. A whip of sand spewed across my face and I shut my eyes. After a while, the noises drifted away.

From somewhere over my head, a fierce argument was being conducted in murderous tones. Dazedly, I tried to make sense of it, but some of the words got lost in my head and others were blown away by the wind.

". . . something with him for God's sake?"

"Go to hell!"

"Sit *down,* Mackin."

There was a slapping noise and some coughing and then the voices loomed larger.

"Jesus Christ, put that thing away."

"Isn't he tough, Sam? Isn't he?"

"Give me the gun, Willy. You hurt Mackin and every stinking cop in the country will be after us."

"That's right," Mackin declared.

"Yeah, but what about the girl, Sam? You said . . ."

"Leave the girl alone," said Mackin furiously. "Or I'll go to the cops myself."

"Like hell you will," shouted Sam. "Sit down, Jesus Christ."

I gathered then that they sat. Though I didn't much care what they did so long as they left me alone. I kept my eyes shut, didn't move, scarcely breathed—just lay there, my mind drifting, trying not to think at all.

I must have slept, for the next I knew the sun was nearly gone and I was shivering. I had been lying on my stomach, arms tucked under me, and they ached as I sat up and blood flowed through them again. My mouth was parched and my throat sore. Gingerly I touched my neck, and wished I hadn't.

Across the desert, the sun was poised just above the Gulf, throwing a red carpet all the way up to the beach. In front of me, not twenty feet away, Sam was trying to build a fire. He was sitting cross-legged on the ground, hacking twigs and bramble with a pen knife, piling them up inside a circle of rocks. Beyond him, Willy lay stretched out, snoring. Mackin, his hands still tied, was lying against the duffle bag staring at me. His mouth was swollen, his right eye red and puffy.

I called to Sam.

"What?" he said irritably.

"I have to go to the bathroom."

"Jesus. Is it necessary?"

"Yes."

He walked over to me with a sigh. "Jesus," he said again. He jerked me to my feet, yelled to Willy, and untied my hands. I stumbled on the rocks as he shoved me rudely in front of him.

The path narrowed and began to wind up the mountain. "Right here, honey." I walked a few feet away from him and trod carefully down a slope. On my left, the mountain fell off gently into a large valley, and beyond rose a second wall of mountains. It was a strange landscape. Two little chains of hills enclosing a valley filled with brush and bramble. Outside the circle, the terrain was barren desert.

I sighed and unzipped my pants.

"Do you realize," said Alexander Mackin, "I could be eating at Antoine's right now?" He stared gloomily into his tin cup. "Where'd you get this shit from, training camp?"

Willy and Sam kept right on eating.

"There's a waiter at Antoine's who knows me," Mackin went on. "He and his brother catch a mess of trout if I call them the day before. Stuff them with crabmeat. *Yetch.*" He put his cup on the ground and turned away from it, as if this rude snub might make it feel contrite.

I dipped the stale bread into the stew and sucked on it. The large pieces of rock disguised as meat wouldn't go down. Just swallowing water had been painful.

"You really should think about going to the shotgun," Sam remarked idly.

"What the hell for?"

"The Cards' defense moves fast. It would buy you time."

"Yeah," said Willy. "It would buy you time."

"I don't need time," Mackin scoffed. "I'm quick." He looked across the fire at me. "Tell them I'm quick, Lindsie. You've done all that research. You should know."

"He's quick," I said. The only way to get rid of the ropes was to pee. But the leather soles and two-inch heels . . . if only I could make it into the valley.

"People think it's all in my arm," Mackin told us. "But it's my reflexes. Haven't lost them yet, either. Have I, Lindsie?"

"He hasn't lost them yet," I supplied and wondered how I could get to Sam's knife. I had seen him put it into his pocket after he had finished making the fire. During the night they would undoubtedly take turns keeping watch. If I could get Sam to crouch down beside me when Willy was sleeping, I could throw sand in his face and go for the knife. I slipped the chocolate bar they had given me into the waist of my pants.

"I still think you should try throwing from the shotgun," said Sam.

Mackin said nothing. Sam shrugged, stood up, and began collecting tin cups. It was dark by then and a cool wind was blowing steadily across the small clearing. Mackin rose. "Gotta take a leak," he announced.

"You take him," Sam told Willy. "And you'd better get the lantern."

"Where is it?"

"I don't know. Try the duffle."

"Hurry it up," said Mackin.

Willy rummaged through the duffle bag, straightened, scratched his head. "Now where did I put that thing? Aw, hell. I must have left it in the jeep."

"Then get it," Sam ordered. "The fire isn't going to last forever. We need the light."

"Are you joking?" said Willy incredulously. "I'll break my neck."

"I'll watch," I offered.

Willy scowled and took several menacing steps toward me.

"Cut it out, honey," Sam said. "Willy?"

"Yeah, yeah. I'm going."

Resignedly, he picked up his jacket and shrugged into it. I could see the bulge in the right-hand pocket made by the gun. Too bad, I thought, as he stomped away.

Or was it?

I glanced speculatively at Mackin. He was standing over the fire staring dreamily into it, his green eyes catching the reflection of the flames. Several feet away, Sam was splashing water from one of the heavy cans into the stew pot; he crouched down and began scrubbing it with paper towels. I glanced back at Mackin. He knew they would kill me. And yet. If they did, and he were returned home—who would blame him? There would probably be a national holiday. Unless I showed up with him. And then there would be a stink.

Sam finished with the pot and stowed it in the duffle. He returned to the fire, crouched down, and began poking at it, trying to keep the flames up until Willy got back.

"Ssss . . ."

I couldn't get his name out. I tried again. Still weak. Stage fright. I cleared my throat. Mackin glanced over at me. His eyes widened.

"Lindsie!" he shouted.

Sam, startled, looked across at me. A blur of movement. His face shot forward. A shower of sparks, hands flew up. Another face, a body on top of his. Flames rose, crackled. The terrified scream ended in a choke.

"Lindsie . . ." he rasped.

I stood on wooden legs, unable to take my eyes off the writhing body, and moved stiffly to where he lay sprawled in the fire. The flames licked at the clumps of hair around his ears and I could smell the burning flesh.

"Goddam, hurry it up," Mackin croaked.

Sam's legs were twitching. His hips were slightly raised over the rocks. Somehow I slipped my hand into his pocket and wrenched out the knife. The moaning was horrible. I cut the ropes around Mackin's wrists. He grabbed the knife from my shaking fingers, and in his frenzy, took a slice of my thumb. I watched the blood seep out as he hacked at my ropes.

"Get the canteen," Mackin said hoarsely.

Sam wasn't moving. My stomach was churning. I found the canteen next to the duffle and picked it up. I stood there not sure what I was supposed to do with it. I spotted the strap of my purse poking out of the duffle. Mindlessly, I grabbed it.

"Come on, Lindsie." Mackin was tugging my arm.

I yanked it free. "No."

"What? For chrissake . . ."

"No," I repeated. "The other way. Willy . . ."

"I know," said Mackin excitedly. "We'll jump him and get the jeep."

I burst out laughing. "You mean," I choked, *bushwack* him?"

"Lindsie."

I staggered past Mackin. "He's got the gun. We'll have to go this way."

We scurried round the side of the mountain, stumbling and bumping into each other, slipping and sliding on the loose stones. We were only a few hundred feet up, but we couldn't see where we were going, and the rubble kept crumbling under our feet. Yet somehow Mackin always kept his balance and seemed annoyed that I did not.

"Couldn't you grab my left arm?" he complained.

"Jesus," I said. "Your arm."

And then, to keep from breaking my neck, I sat down and slid the rest of the way to the bottom.

"Okay," said Mackin eagerly. "Now we backtrack around the mountain and take off the way we came. I've got it all figured out."

I pulled off my shoes and dumped out half of Pico Johnson.

"For such a terrific quarterback, Alex, your strategy stinks. All Willy has to do is get in the jeep and he'd find us right away."

"I suppose you have a better idea?"

"Right. We walk across this valley and cut through those mountains on the other side. That way he can't follow in the jeep. Then we'll angle off to the left a bit and hope we can make it back to the brush before daylight, back to where the cabin is. Once we're that far, he'll never find us from the road."

Mackin was a pretty good quarterback after all.

He knew when his coach was right.

_______________________ **_Chapter 17_**

Tall, spooky shapes rose up before us. Long, bony hands
darted out of the night to rake shoulders, claw faces. Sharp-
toothed mesquite grabbed ankles. And the crisp snapping of
twigs, the crunching of stones, sent things crawling down my
spine—and probably scurrying from under my feet. It was
Halloween night, full moon and all, and lurching somewhere in
the valley . . . was Ichabod Crane.

He could have been anywhere.

The valley floor, which had looked to be roughly one mile
across and flat, was nothing of the sort. Maybe a mile, maybe
twenty, but certainly not flat. No two square inches seemed to
share the same altitude, and the upwards and downwards were
nastily camouflaged by thick brush and vicious plants. And still
the mountains we were heading for stood unbudgingly where
they were.

After an hour of climbing, ducking, tripping, stumbling,
swearing aloud, I grudgingly revised my opinion of Mackin's
plan. But, of course, it was too late.

Suddenly Mackin stopped and turned. His face white in the
moonlight. "Hear anything?"

I came up beside him and listened. Hearing nothing, I heard
everything. "Do you?"

He craned his neck and glanced nervously over my shoulder.
"I think Willy's back there," he said tensely.

I turned and searched the darkness for movement. I could

_141_

feel Mackin's breath on the back of my neck. It gave me goose-bumps. At any moment I expected to hear a shot and the chilling sound of Willy's high-pitched laughter.

"Let's not find out," I said.

It became a thought process. Right foot. Left foot. Big step. Baby step. Mother, may I? Duck down. Catch up to Mackin's disappearing back, never knowing what was behind mine. Going on like this, until suddenly, Mackin wasn't there any-more.

I had come to a thick wall of brush and I couldn't see him anywhere. It was ghostly quiet. I took a few steps round to the right and saw how the ground began to rise. Back around to the left I found a small opening and ducked into it. The light from the moon didn't penetrate and I was feeling my way blindly, using my hands to push back the brush. Up ahead I could see a small clearing . . . and then he grabbed me.

"Jesus," I croaked.

"I think I heard something."

"So did I," I said with a shiver. "My heart just stopped."

Mackin was jabbing the air frantically. "Over there," he whispered.

"There?" He was pointing straight ahead. "But Willy couldn't have . . ."

"No," said Mackin gruffly. "But it could be a snake." He turned and looked at me accusingly. "Do you have any idea what's crawling around down here?"

"Headless horsemen?"

"It's not funny." He shuddered.

He had twigs in his hair and his eyes were enormous. He was clutching the canteen almost desperately. I laughed. "Come on, Alex. You're not the squeamish type."

The green eyes narrowed. "You won't catch me walking into any snakes."

"You're afraid of snakes?"

"Damn right," he said with feeling. "I'm afraid of anything that crawls or flies."

"But not things that have trunks?"

"That's different," he said stiffly. "You can outsmart mammals."

I sighed. "I'd rather try to outsmart a reptile," I told him, "than a mammal with a gun. Let's go."

He grinned. "You first."

It was nearly eleven by the time we reached the base of the mountains. I collapsed on the ground and gingerly removed my shoes. A large watery blister had formed under my right big toe. Another one had snuck in between my little and fourth toes. The left foot had a blister under the middle toe and something shaped like Cuba on the heel. I probed them gently.

"You were wrong," said Mackin suddenly. "I shouldn't have listened to you."

"It was a mistake," I agreed.

"Christ, we could have been home by now."

"I'm sorry," I said with mild apology. "Will you help me with these blisters?"

"What do you want me to do . . . hold them?

I set my foot carefully on the ground and looked up at Mackin. He seemed to be glaring at me and then I realized that he wasn't seeing me at all. "Alex, what's wrong?"

He blinked, saw me, scowled. "What's wrong?" he said bitterly. "I just fucking killed a man."

"You mustn't think about that now," I sighed.

"If you hadn't come," he went on "none of this would have happened."

"I didn't kidnap you," I said quietly.

"Well I didn't kidnap me either. Or do you think I'm in on it, too?"

"Maybe just a little bit," I said.

"Right," he snapped. "They kidnap me then give me a share of the ransom. It's called a gratuity."

"Maybe just a little more," I suggested.

Mackin gave me a small wintry smile. "Then you don't know everything, do you? High rollers are big tippers."

"Alex . . ."

"Do you realize," he said pointing a finger at me, "that I don't even know who you are?"

It seemed an odd thing to say and I wasn't sure how to reply, so I just sat there and watched him walk in aimless little circles, until eventually he got it worked out of him and came over and sat down.

He shook his head. "I'm sorry, Lindsie. But, Jesus, I killed the bastard."

"I know, Alex, but we've got to keep moving."

Mackin nodded. "Do you have a match?"

"A lighter."

"Okay."

I dug my lighter out of my purse and handed it to him. He flicked it on and began passing the tip of Sam's knife through the flame.

"Will you be gentle?" I said.

Mackin grunted and reached for my foot. He began operating on my right big toe. "There's not much water . . . don't move."

"Then what's all that gunk?"

"In the canteen. It's only half-full."

"That's nice," I said and began to compute. The average person lost five and a half quarts of water a day. Under normal circumstances. Even subtracting the two quarts urinated, that still left almost a gallon. And in the desert you probably needed close to two for replacement. I couldn't be sure because that survival school I had done a story on had been in cool, green Colorado, not brown, arid Mexico. Which hardly mattered.

The canteen looked to hold no more than a quart. "Ouch."

"You got a bandaid?" asked Mackin.

"And foot powder, too."

"Well how the hell do I know what you've got stashed in that thing? Never mind." He pulled up his windbreaker and began tearing strips from his shirt. "We'll tie one around the big toe," he said matter-of-factly, "and we'll line your shoes with bits of material to absorb the sweat. How come women wear such dumb shoes anyway?"

"Beats me," I said.

I watched the way his hands moved as he fixed up my toe and carefully placed the pieces of ragged material in my shoes. "There," he said at last. "You're in business. May I escort you out of the desert, ma'am?"

"Sure, Moses. Let's go."

We didn't go far. After two hours of slipping and sliding, we had climbed only halfway up the shallowest ridge. Unfortunately, the shallowest ridge soared more than it sloped. "I think," I said wearily, "that even if I make it up, I'll never make it back down."

Mackin was standing just above me, balancing on two widely spaced rocks. He got both his feet on one, and handed me up to the other. We stood there looking bleakly above us.

"If we wait until morning," I went on, "at least we'll be able to see." The moon had drifted behind us so that our bodies threw dark shadows ahead of us.

"I guess," said Mackin, toying with his mustache, "But let's see if we can at least get to the top. We can't stay here."

"No." I was so tired, I could hardly move. My legs ached and my blisters were reproducing with abandon. Getting to the top of the ridge was going to be rough, because from this point on, the angle of incline rose sharply. I took off my blazer and tied the sleeves around my waist to give me more flexibility.

"Here," said Mackin, "let me take your purse. It'll leave your arms free."

He hung both my purse and the canteen around his neck. "You go first," he said encouragingly, "in case you slip."

We inched our way up cautiously, Mackin doing one of his pep talk routines, which failed to inspire me at all. After every move, I had to stop, search for a new foothold, lift one leg up to it, reach for a rock or a crevice above me, and slowly pull myself up. My legs were beginning to wobble and my hands were scratched and bleeding. Finally, when we appeared close to the top, I stopped once again to catch my breath. The final stretch was nothing more than a sheer face of solid rock. In the dim light, I could see no handhold, no foothold. Mackin edged up next to me and surveyed the situation.

"Okay," he said, "there's a dent just above your head. Can you make it?"

"I can't even *see* it."

"I'll give you a leg up," he said cheerfully. "Just throw yourself against the rock and you can work your hand over to it."

I looked at him in disbelief.

"Come on, Lindsie, you can do it." His eyes were calm and he was smiling. But then, he was used to sending people out on kamikazi missions.

My stomach knotted. "No."

He put his arm around my shoulders and grinned. With his black eye and scruffy beard he looked like a pirate. "Look, Hollis, it's third and long and if we can make this yardage, it'll be fourth and goal and we'll run a double zigout and . . ."

"Oh, God."

"Lindsie, we can't just stay here."

I tilted my head back and looked at the sheet of rock. I felt dizzy. "Couldn't you just pass me?" I moaned.

"Look, this was your idea."

"All right," I said. "But will you do me a favor? I have this parakeet and, well, he's sort of like my best friend, and would you make sure he finds a nice home?"

Mackin smiled. "No. But I will promise to get you home. Here."

He cupped his hands.

"My heel," I said.

"That's okay."

I hiked my leg up and set my heel in his hands. Then I pushed off the ground with my right foot and caught the side of the mountain with the flat of my hands. I let my body fall forward until I was plastered against the rock. I could hear Mackin breathing under me.

"Okay," he said, "now reach up to your right, slowly . . . that's it. A little more. Couple more inches. Got it?"

"Yes." I gulped. What I'd got was three fingers in a dent.

"Okay, now move your right foot to the right of you, there's a small rock jutting out . . . *no.* Back a bit, there."

I could feel his hands wobbling. "I'm coming down," I said.

"No, you're not. Now look to your left and try to find something to grip. You're doing great. I bet you do this all the time."

I could feel the sweat on my face and a faint breeze blowing through my hair. Cautiously, I reached out with my left hand and began groping for anything I could sink my fingers into. His hands kept wobbling. I pressed my cheek against the cold stone and leaned harder into the mountain hoping to transfer some of my weight to it. I could feel my breath coming back at me from the rock and was also aware of a small sobbing sound rising from deep down inside me.

Mackin seemed to be saying something but all my concentration was in my groping fingertips. Finally I found a tiny space between two rocks just big enough to shove my fingers into. The stone was rough and hostile as if it were trying to push my fingers away. I gripped it more tightly and closed my eyes, trying to catch my breath. Mackin's arms were shaking badly. I had to move. Timidly, I raised my left foot before he could drop it.

"Now what?" I breathed.

"I can't see that far. Just keep pushing into the rock with your body and then feel above you with your right hand. Don't worry about falling, cause I'm right here."

I couldn't move. They should have let Willy strangle me, I thought, it would have been quicker. I was close to panic. I could feel all the tension of my muscles and my fear bottled up inside me ready to explode. I had to do something before it all broke and I let go. Mucus from my nose dribbled onto my lip.

I lifted my right hand and began feeling above me. I discovered an opening about two feet over my head. Pushing up onto my right toe, I carefully explored the opening with my hand. It seemed to be a deep crevice, but I couldn't reach high enough to tell how wide it was. I squeezed it to see if it would crumble. It didn't. I gripped it as tightly as I could and worked my left hand up to it. When I had both hands grasping it, I began walking my left foot up. But as I got to the point where I had to start transfering weight—my foot slipped. Had to get the shoe off, I thought frantically. But my damp foot was sticking to the cloth Mackin had laid in there. For him to help me with it, I would have to work my way down from the ledge. My arms were beginning to ache from being over my head so long.

With my right foot planted precariously on the small bump, I gradually raised my left leg, brought my left hand down and jerkily removed the shoe. I set it on the ledge and placed my bare foot against the mountain. The cold stone felt good against my sore toes. I pushed hard against them and down on my hands and slowly raised myself up until my head was even with the ledge, and then I brought my left knee up and balanced like a tripod.

The crevice was a half-open mouth, no more than two feet deep, the roof of it just high enough for me to slip inside. I lowered my head and propelled myself into it, wiggling around until I was lying flat. Something small scurried out.

I lay there panting and still shaking, feeling the cold jagged rocks beneath my cheek. I could see out across the valley to the other string of mountains, the moon hanging up there like a fly ball in the split second before it begins to come down. And I was suddenly struck by the cold indifference of the environment. You could cajole, you could beg, you could plead. It would not help you. Instead, the environment seemed to fight you, setting up inexorable challenges that you had to meet with your brain and your body. The tools of survival in the city— money, credit cards, telephones, taxi cabs, people—had no meaning out here. I was overcome, not with fear, but with awe, and a profound sense of loneliness that I could mean so little.

Somewhere below, Mackin was calling. And for a moment, I resented his intrusion. I wanted to be by myself for a while longer. Suddenly it seemed important that I figure out how to relate to the environment. I wanted to be a part of it, to comprehend it, and Mackin was trying to drag me back to that other world. I didn't move.

He called again.

"Lindsie?"

I sighed, and managed to roll onto my side, at the same time swinging my legs out over the ledge. Then I peered down. I couldn't see him. I twisted my head and studied the rocky incline above me. I put my shoe back on, raised my left arm and swiveled onto my left knee. Facing into the crevice, I stretched out my right leg and dragged myself sideways onto the rocks.

I got my feet now under me and crawled the remaining ten feet to the top.

"Okay," I yelled. "I'm up."

I still couldn't see Mackin. It was deathly still and definitely spooky, with just the gentle breezes blowing across the desert and the big bright stars spattering the sky. I began to shiver, but I was too exhausted to untie the sleeves of my blazer and put it on. I sat there, waiting.

"Alex?"

I got slowly to my feet and discovered I was not at the top of the mountain after all. I was standing in a shallow pit. Off to my right, the mountain rose to its final peak. I walked across the pit and up the other side and found that, thankfully, from there it sloped down to the flat desert floor, so we wouldn't have to climb any higher. I went back to the other side.

"Alex? Are you there?" Still no reply.

I crept down a couple of feet. I didn't want to go all the way back to the ledge. It wasn't big enough to hold two people, and God only knew how much weight it would take. These rubbly old mountains were too infirm to hold even themselves up. I squinted again at the left corner of the ledge. One groping hand slithered onto it.

"Almost," I said encouragingly. "The ledge is wide enough to crawl into." I could hear him grunting.

Gradually, he hoisted himself up, crawled onto the ledge and collapsed. The panting became interspersed with some pretty foul language.

"I think I'll just stay here and petrify," he declared. "I'll shove my face out and they can call it Mt. Mackmore."

"After all the trouble I went through to get us a room?"

"Very funny."

"I'm serious. You'll love the decor. It's not exactly early jungle and there aren't any waterbeds with spiffy red hearts, but it does have a nice view.

He looked up at me suspiciously. "How do you know about my sheets?"

"I won't tell until you come up."

"Jesus." Sighing and grumbling, Mackin dragged himself out of the crevice and climbed the last few feet to the top.

"See," I said gesturing, "the penthouse at the Plaza."

He rubbed his hand across his face and cleared his throat. "Then it sure has gone downhill."

"Is that supposed to be funny?"

His gaze returned to me. "How come," he said, "in the movies the guy always gets stranded with a beautiful woman?"

"You're not exactly Prince Charming."

"That's cause I'm still a frog."

"I thought you looked a little green."

"At least the view's nice."

"The Plaza," I agreed.

He rubbed his mustache thoughtfully and glanced around the pit. "What, no shower?"

"I'll phone room service," I said. "Champagne?"

"Right. Dom Perignon 'fifty-five."

"Did you happen to notice the room number?"

Mackin sat down on a pile of rocks. "Heaven," he sighed. "Just tell them to send it to heaven." We burst out laughing.

For some reason, it seemed terribly funny.

**Chapter 18**

Our laughter rang hollow in the desert night, and as the echoes died away, so did our forced gaiety.

Mackin pulled off his shoes and socks and gave his feet a thorough examination. I sat down across from him and rummaged through my purse for a brush. But my scalp was still sore from Willy yanking my hair, so I gave up and dug around for my cigarettes. Came across the candy bar and couldn't remember how it had gotten there. I hesitated, my fingers touching the paper. Reluctantly, I pushed it aside, found the cigarettes and carefully counted each one. Seven. Lit one and inhaled the smoke deeply. It tasted good.

I leaned back against the pit and smoked in silence. Mackin had put on his shoes and socks and was massaging his right shoulder. I wondered what he was thinking, what had motivated him to do it. Greed? Egotism? That he had gotten away with so much and thought he could do anything? Perhaps Chip had been right when he said that Mackin had created the legend as protection against the insanity of hero worship. He lived in an image of his own making—the outrageous, egotistical superstar—so he could preserve a small piece of himself. But somewhere along the line, he had started believing the legend and had been consumed by it. And now he was stuck.

I stubbed out my cigarette, too weary to think anymore. He was now working on his left shoulder, kneading and prodding the muscles, rolling his head slowly from side to side, his ragged shirttails hanging out of his jacket. He noticed me watching him and straightened.

"What?" he asked.

"Just thinking."

"What?"

"Why you did it . . . fixed that Super Bowl game."

"Mm." Mackin screwed up his face and began probing his bruised eye. "Suppose I tell you there was no fix?"

"Just because the NFL cleared you . . ."

Mackin pressed the lid closed and looked at me with one eye. "But don't you see?" he said eagerly. "They wouldn't have if they hadn't been absolutely sure. You should know that."

"I know it's impossible to fault a quarterback for an interception," I said mildly.

"Not that time," he said cheerfully. "It was a damn bad play. I should have had it and I blew it."

"And got paid handsomely for it, too."

Mackin looked at me with both eyes. "Oh, that's terrific, Lindsie. Have you found the bloody axe from that Hollywood rape-murder, too? It's under my bed." He smiled sourly. "That's why my sheets have bleeding hearts on them."

I sighed. "Alex, they asked you to keep the spread under ten and you did."

"Right," he snapped. "Before you can become a quarterback in the NFL you have to go to computer school."

"Then you explain it."

Mackin shook his head wearily. "It's too complicated to go into. But it isn't what you think." He looked at me with large, beseeching eyes.

"Lindsie, believe me, I didn't fix it. I . . . couldn't."

I looked at him and said nothing. I wanted to believe him innocent. Maybe it was nothing more than the sexuality. Maybe it was because deep down inside football ran deeper than I would admit or, more simply, because I still wanted to believe there could be heroes. But if I discounted all that, I could see all too well an ingenious man lying through his teeth in the hope of saving a career.

He had already lied to me once, telling me his legs were going, thinking nobody would believe that except maybe a dumb girl reporter. Then he called me Lucy, and I had said it was Lindsie Hollis, and when he asked how I knew about Sammy Hines, I had said I had grown up in Chicago—and it had clicked. And he saw how he could use me. The fear of dying had been merely a cover, Mackin's cover, a way out of his jam. It was just wild enough to be believed by the press, especially coming from Jason Hollis' daughter. But more cleverly, the blackmailers would see it for the warning it was.

"Do you know," said Mackin, sitting down beside me, "that you were incredible out there?"

"It's the desert," I said.

"Yes," he agreed. "It brings out a kind of fury in you because you feel so helpless. I found myself talking to the mountain, threatening it, cursing it, pleading, trying to make it accept me. And nothing. There's no way to get through to it or to beat it. You can only use evasive tactics. Do you know what I mean?"

"Yes," I said. And now he was telling me, just as persuasively as he had that night, that he was innocent. Thinking perhaps he could still save his career. For who would believe what a desperate kidnapper said?

". . . And it made me realize how everything I have at home is so meaningless. It's just phony security, do you realize that, Lindsie? We call it progress, but it's just a social lie. Because when man is really threatened, whether it's by the environment or nature or sickness or even another man, all those material things don't count. It's just you that has to fight. And if you lose, it really doesn't make any difference. It's scary."

"I know." It would be Dion's word against Mackin's. Unless I wrote my story.

He turned and I could feel his eyes on me. "Do you know what else? Here we are, two people who don't even know each other, and yet we need each other more than we've ever needed anybody." A pause. "That's weird."

"I sure could do with some champagne," I said.

Mackin laughed. "Sorry. I didn't mean to sound like Plato. Hell, you don't even have your notebook out." He tapped my knee. "Why don't you have your notebook out?"

I smiled and rested my head on his shoulder. He had no idea, I thought, what tomorrow was going to be like. He could only marvel at what he had been through tonight. Ridiculously, I began to feel sorry for him. And suddenly, I didn't care what he had or hadn't done. I was weary of my own cynicism, tired of always searching for motives, loopholes, lies. I was bored with listening to myself think. For once I needed something to believe in; I needed a rest from *me*.

I found myself snuggling closer to him and feeling the hard muscles of his shoulder under the nylon jacket as he shifted and brought his arm around me. I slid my cheek higher up onto his shoulder and then, slowly, it began to dawn on me.

"Alex?"

"Mm?"

"Take off your jacket. I want to try something."

"Me too."

I smiled. "What we're going to try is to make water."

"I thought you wanted champagne."

"I don't know how to make champagne, but I do know about water." Thanks to Maxwell and his silly survival story.

Mackin pulled the jacket over his head. "You just wave it over the canteen and it multiplies?"

I laughed. "Yes. But first you dig a hole and put a tin cup in the ground."

"Unhuh . . ."

"And then you stretch a piece of plastic or nylon over the hole, weight down the edges with rocks, and put a rock right in the middle over the cup."

"And because the air is warmer in the hole," said Mackin, "it condenses and produces drops of water on the underside of the jacket, right?"

"Right. And with the rock weighting down the middle, the jacket funnels the water into the cup."

"And I suppose you just happen to have a tin cup with you?"

I shook my head. "We'll have to use the canteen."

"You're sure the water won't evaporate?"

"Not at night. Let's try it."

With cold, stiff fingers we began pawing at the rocks and gravel in the deepest part of the pit. Got the hole dug, uncapped the canteen, set it inside. "It's called a water still," I explained, placing rocks around the edges of Mackin's jacket. "Every good Boy Scout should know how to make one."

We finished and sat back shivering. The moon was lower in the sky and I could hear Mackin's soft breathing beside me.

"Somehow," he said, "I can't quite picture you a Boy Scout."

"A Girl Scout then?"

"Maybe. But you didn't learn that in Girl Scouts."

"You should know," I teased, "that I do my homework. When I was assigned this story I ran out and took a course on desert survival."

Mackin began toying with his mustache. "Is that so?"

"Yes."

"And did they teach you how to keep warm?"

I nodded. "They taught us how to start a fire without matches. But I sort of flunked that part."

"Good," declared Mackin. "Because I know a way to keep warm and it generally works."

"Really?"

"Shall I show you?"

I ran my finger across the back of his hand. "Else I won't believe you."

He brought his arms up and then I was tasting his mouth, a long slow sticky kiss that went down just fine. "I want you to believe me," he said huskily. "I really do."

"Then you must stop twirling your mustache," I murmured. "Like a villain."

"I will," he promised. "I will."

And then it was just the three of us, Mackin, me, and the mountain. Feeling his mustache brushing my lip as I worked my way through it until I found his mouth. Floating, feeling nothing, not even my body, or his. Just his mouth. And a rock. A soft moan. I was hurting his mouth.

Trying to be gentle, feeling the roughness of his beard, the soft skin, the hard muscles . . . feeling the sensation down to my toes. The sensation of heat and wanting and another sharp rock, and gravel.

Shifting, squirming, slipping my hand between us, feeling the taut muscles of his stomach and then . . . I forgot the mountain and the stones. And the scary Ichabod Crane night.

"You promised you wouldn't hurt me," said Mackin shaking me awake.

I sat up quickly and looked around. The desert had turned from black to gray and a thin mist was climbing up the mountains. I glanced at my watch. Six-twenty. I yawned and looked down at Mackin who was rubbing his shoulder.

"I'm sorry," I said formally. "You should have wakened me."

He smiled weakly. "That's okay. It needed to be put out

of its misery anyway."

"What's wrong with your arm?"

He grimaced. "The climb, the cold air. It needs to be kept at seventy-two degrees at night." He squeezed his shoulder furiously. "And then, it hasn't had its daily massage in what? A week?" He stared at it sadly.

In the gray dawn, he looked awful. The ragged dark beard, swollen right eye, puffy mouth, dirt streaked all over his torn shirt. I smiled, wondering how awful I looked. I didn't have to wonder how awful I felt. Stiff and aching. Mouth like sand.

"You could at least stay with me until the sun's up," he complained, as I hobbled over to the canteen. I removed the rocks, tossed him his jacket, and lifted the metal container.

"Well?"

I shook it carefully. "Feels a little heavier," I said. "Maybe another cup or so." I brought the canteen over to him and we each had a swallow. But when I handed him my candy bar he shook his head, reached into his back pocket, and produced one of his own.

"What else?" I asked suspiciously.

"How did you know?"

"I heard something crinkling."

From his other pocket he removed a squished package of raisins. I reached for them.

"Not so fast," said Mackin. "I keep the raisins. That way you'll have to be nice to me."

"I tried," I told him. "But I only ended up hurting you."

He broke his candy bar in two. "Then you'll just have to try harder . . . mm . . . that's much better."

Picking our way down the backside of the mountain proved even tougher than grappling up it. Whereas going up, you could use the forward thrust of your body, coming down you had to depend on your legs alone. And my legs were shot.

I had no traction in my soles and as the sun climbed slowly in the sky, something began to give inside me as I felt once again the awesome pull of the desert. The indignant fury it had brought out the night before had chilled . . . into a slow, numbing resignation.

It was after eight by the time we hit bottom, the sun an indistinct blur in the still colorless sky. Eight, and already I was sick with thirst. I sat down and pulled off my shoes and stared out across all that sand, and knew then I wasn't going make it.

Mackin crouched down beside me. "At least it's flat," he said without enthusiasm.

Flat and burning, I thought.

"How far do you suppose we have to go?"

I shrugged.

"Maybe," he said slowly, "we ought to circle back and wait for them. We can hide in the brush and try to jump them. You can use the knife and I'm not a bad fighter."

I turned and glanced at his beat up face but said nothing.

Mackin sighed. "I suppose you're not too keen on using a knife though."

"No," I said. "I'm not too keen."

"Then what?"

I licked my lips. They felt like sandpaper. "Either we go now and try to beat our way across the desert by noon, or we wait until they've gone, or . . ."

"Or what?"

I stared at all the gunk seeping out of my blisters. "I don't know. Maybe I'll just stay here."

"Are you crazy?" said Mackin incredulously.

"They won't hurt you."

"For God's sake, Lindsie."

"You can leave me the water and the raisins and when you

get back to San Diego you could get somebody to come fetch me."

"You mean," he said angrily, "before I fly off to New Orleans? Or should I wait until I throw a couple of touchdowns, call time out, and rush off on a white horse?"

"A Charger," I agreed.

"Dammit, Lindsie, you've got to learn to trust somebody sometime. The only person you trust is yourself."

I met his angry eyes. "I don't trust anybody, Alex, who goes around fooling people for fun."

"No? Well what about you? You con people, too. You take whatever you can get from them for your goddam news stories. But what do you ever give back?"

"That's not fair," I said grudgingly.

"Sure it is," replied Mackin. "What you are comes out in what you do. You wouldn't be a reporter if you weren't ambitious, distrustful, and selfish. Like me." He leaned over and looked at my watch. "Lessee, if we walk four miles an hour we could make fourteen, fifteen miles. You think it's more than that?"

"I didn't count," I said, still angry that he had touched a raw nerve.

"Goddammit," he said harshly. "We're going to get out of this lousy desert, together, alive. And don't tell me you can't do it. Can't is only the head. So do you want to go now or wait until noon? And hurry it up."

Beneath his anger I sensed a note of panic.

"You're the quarterback," I said quietly.

"And you're the coach, Coach."

"Coach goes with quarterback."

"One hundred percent?"

". . . All right."

"Then let's go."

I felt relieved that he had made the decision. I didn't want to be wrong again. Only problem was, this time Mackin was wrong.

We hadn't walked a hundred yards when we heard the low, unmistakable rumble of an engine.

**Chapter 19**

"You've got to understand how it was. You've got to get inside my head. You've got to remember how it was then."

He had gone into that season six years ago determined to win the Super Bowl. To anyone but him it would have sounded preposterous. The young team Harley Crittenden had fashioned two years before was no more than a fluke, football people were sure. There was Mackin, of course, and Austin Holbrook at middle lineback, and Chip Tobias at halfback, all promising third-year men signed out of college as part of Crittenden's desperate plan to turn around his failing franchise. There had been others. Crittenden had traded, sold, or released 15 of his aging starters; he had even supplied a new coach, Charlie Sims out of Tulane, and a new team slogan, "We've been re-Charged!"

And they were, more or less. With more exuberance than expertise, the San Diego Chargers actually finished that first season with a 7–6–1 record. Mackin, of course, became the town's new hero. Everybody waited for next year.

It was a joke. With a single game over Oakland, the Chargers won their division, despite a shoulder separation that kept Mackin out nearly half the season. And then came the AFC title match against the wild card Raiders that sent everyone home nodding their heads knowingly. The Chargers blew it, 42 to 13; they had been a fluke, of course, what else? Nobody waited for next year.

Except Mackin. That spring he spent six weeks closeted with Sims learning to read defenses, studying game films hour after bleary hour. Another six weeks working on running plays with Chip and passing patterns with wide receiver Hilton Jones. And by the time training camp opened, he knew he had it.

And he did. That year Mackin set the record for most touchdown passes in a single season and led his team to its first conference title in seven years. His face grinned out from the cover of every major national magazine. In Washington, the President announced he would personally attend the Super Bowl; America needed young men like Alex Mackin.

"You've got to understand how it was. I was only twenty-four and I was a national celebrity. Do you know what it's like to have the President calling you and famous actresses draping themselves all over your apartment? I had everything. Money, women, fame. And you should have seen the way I was throwing that ball. Check back, you'll see! Hell, some of my passes just went on forever. And they were perfect, right on the numbers every time. I could do anything. I was twenty-four and I was making all those older guys look ridiculous because it was so easy. Do you know that quarterbacks don't even begin to peak until they're thirty?

"I was so high that season I could hardly sleep. Actually, it's amazing I made it through the year at all, because I did an awful lot of stupid things. It was like my head stopped working and I was just tearing around like one of those crazy wind-up toys. It's kind of funny thinking back on it because that guy Mackin, hell, I don't even know him any more. It's like talking about someone else.

"Anyway, that's the way it was before the Super Bowl. And believe me, it wasn't just me, we were all like that. A bunch of crazy, hyped-up kids who didn't know their heads from their asses. So there we were in Miami one night, I'm sitting on the bed going over the Cowboys' defenses and Chip's watching the tube, when the phone rings. I grab it and this guy says, 'Alex Mackin?'

"Sure is, I say.

"His name is Smith, he says, and he represents a business consortium, those are his exact words, and he believed he could offer me and Chip an opportunity to make a lot of money. I say that's fine and why doesn't he get in touch with our agents after the Super Bowl? And he, real politely, says he's sorry to bother us, but that his associates need to know right away if we'd be interested. If we weren't, he says, they would try to get Billy Joe Morris of the Cowboys. He said they needed to make some kind of announcement before the game or the deal would fall through, and could Chip and I possibly meet him for a quick drink?

"Well, there I'd been all week, working up a real fine hate for Billy Joe and the thought of him getting some hotdog deal sent me right up the wall. I said where? He said to meet him at Horace's Bar on Collins Avenue at nine-thirty.

"Okay, so we get to Horace's, order a beer, and wait. Pretty soon it gets to be ten and no one's come over to us. Our curfew, by the way, is eleven. So I go up to the bartender and ask if anybody named Smith is looking for me. He says not that he knows of. We order another round and about ten minutes later the bartender comes over and says a man just called and left word that a limousine would pick us up out front in five minutes . . . *no wait.* It gets better!

"Sure enough this black limo rolls up and the chauffeur gets out, comes around, opens the back door and asks us to step inside. Chip climbs in first, then me. There's a solid sheet of glass between the front and back seat. And there's this guy sitting up front with a big hat on and sunglasses. He doesn't turn around. The chauffeur gets in and we drive off. Chip and

I are looking at each other and wondering what the hell is going on. We go maybe two blocks and all of a sudden there's this *voice*.

"It says, 'Mr. Mackin, Mr. Tobias, it's a pleasure to meet you. Please don't be alarmed. We are merely going to drive a bit. There is, you will notice, an intercom attached to the back of the front seat. If you will just flick the switch when you wish to speak, I will be able to hear you. You will also notice the buttons on the doors are *up,* so that at any time you may ask the driver to stop and you may leave the car. Please flick the switch now, Mr. Mackin, and tell me if I should continue.'

"Well, Chip and I are sitting there with our jaws on the floor, but I figure, what the hell? So I lean over and flick the switch and say go ahead, just as long as we get back by eleven.

"The deal, he says, is this. He represents a group of ten wealthy men who want to invest in the team. The Chargers, he says, are picked to win the Super Bowl by ten but he and his partners are pretty sure we can take it by thirteen. Did we think that was a fair assessment?

" 'Well,' I say, 'you can never tell about these things, but could you get to the point?'

" 'What we want,' he says, 'is insurance that you won't beat the spread. Keep the win under ten points and you can split $50,000.'

"Chip and I broke up. Thought it was the funniest thing we ever heard. Then I notice it's ten to eleven and we're on the highway to Lauderdale. So I switch on the intercom and say, 'Sure, man, no problem. Just make the payment in old bills, nothing bigger than hundreds.'

"He turns and says something to the driver and all you can see is that big hat and the sunglasses and suddenly the whole thing is so ludicrous that we start laughing all over again. Some goddamn fan, I'm thinking, who's going to go home and brag around the office how he's fixed the Super Bowl.

"We get back to the hotel and he says he'll be in touch. And we get out of the car with our sides splitting.

"The next night Chip and I are having dinner at the Carriage House and we start talking about the man. Every so often Chip stretches up and looks toward the door and says, 'Say, Mack, you see any limousines out there?' And we break up. And we're dreaming up these plays on how to blow important downs. Like the Six Thousand Dollar Sack and the Fortune Fumble and stuff like that. Well, I guess that's when Sixten Sizemore overheard us talking.

"Anyway, it wasn't until late in the second period after we'd scored a couple of times that I remembered the man. I swear, after that night at dinner, I don't think we ever thought about it again what with all the meetings and parties and media stuff. But there I was in the biggest game of my life, a game I'd dreamt about since I was a kid, and Christ, it was so easy! We were rolling over those Cowboys like they were pygmies. And I'm thinking, jeez, this is a drag. It's *boring.* It's disappointing! This is the celebrated Super Bowl? What a laugh. I guess that's when I began thinking about the fix. Could I do it? Christ, what a trip that would be! Fixing a goddamn Super Bowl. Nobody, but nobody, had ever done that.

"Mind you, it was just a passing thought. Then they blew that pass into the end zone and suddenly I knew I was going to try it. What was there to lose? Even if they scored twice, I could score again. I could do anything, right? But I knew I couldn't just start missing. So when I got hit in the third quarter, I faked an ankle injury. I remember sitting on the bench trying not to laugh. It was all so easy."

The silence was unnerving. High above, the sun threw off its scorching rays. An electric blue horsefly hovered lazily overhead, rising straight up, drifting back down like a helicopter caught up in turbulence. I lit up my first cigarette of the day and pretended I was breathing in water. We had been lying flat on the ground for almost two and a half hours, ever since we had raced back to the mountain at the sound of the approaching engine. With not a second to spare we had managed to lose ourselves in the high brush just as the Volkswagen Thing rumbled into view with an intent-looking Willy hunched over the wheel.

As soon as he was well beyond us, we had slithered back up the mountain, until we found a small flat space that seemed to offer good cover. From there we watched Willy zigzag recklessly back and forth around the base of the mountains until, at last, he had bounced out of sight, presumably back to the other ring of hills. We hadn't had a chance to take him. And now we were forced to wait.

I tried to pay attention to what Mackin was saying, but my thoughts kept drifting—as far as the eye could see.

"So I'm sitting on the bench and the Cowboys score and it's like somebody throwing water in my face. What am I doing? I say to myself. This is the *Super Bowl,* what am I doing on the bench?

"Next thing I know I'm plunging back in just crying to get another touchdown. I swear, Lindsie, I totally forgot the goddamn fix. I just wanted to score. Two wasn't enough. I wanted three. I wanted everybody to know that it was me, Alex Mackin, who had won the Super Bowl.

"That's why, when we got down to the fifteen, I went over and argued with Sims. He wanted to set up the field goal. But I wanted the touchdown. Besides, the wind was really blowing in and I honestly figured we'd have a better chance throwing a low pass. I told him if I didn't think I could do it, I would throw off to the side and White would still be in good position to kick. Sims finally agreed. I took the snap and I moved back.

I thought I had time. The pocket felt safe. You get a feel for these things, almost a sixth sense. Chip wasn't clear yet. I kept moving back, didn't feel rushed. And then, just as I was throwing, I got blasted. I didn't even know who the hell hit me until I got up. I've relived that play a hundred times and I still don't know how that linebacker got through.

"Anyway, I got all caught up in the celebration and I was invited to have dinner with the President and I must have been freaked out for about two weeks. Crittenden signed me to a new three-year contract and I had all those offers to be in commercials and I stopped thinking about the pass and never did give another thought to the fix."

"Until they came with the money," I said.

"Yeah."

"Sam brought it to you. Wrapped in brown paper. And you took it."

"Sure I took it," said Mackin. "I didn't know what the hell it was. This was about a month after the game and this guy just comes up to the door and hands it to me. 'What's this?' I say.

" 'Have fun,' he says and leaves.

"So I open it up and there's a stack of hundred dollar bills. I start counting. Five hundred of them. I sit there in a daze, thinking fifty thousand dollars? What the hell? Then it dawns on me. The weirdo in the limo had said fifty thousand. Jesus Christ, I think, if anybody ever finds out about this, I'm dead. I've got to tell them I didn't do it. Got to return the money. But how? I don't even know who they are. So I figure I'll just hide the money and maybe they'll try to contact me again."

"But why a checking account?" I said. "Why not a safe deposit box?"

"Or a Swiss account?" he said sardonically. "Look, I'm not a criminal. I don't think like that. All I knew was I wanted to get the damn money out of my sight. Besides, what if I dropped dead and they opened it up? Look kind of suspicious, don't you think?"

We were wedged into the side of the mountain, lying flat on our stomachs under some low branches out of the direct rays of the sun. It wasn't that hot, maybe eighty degrees, and lying in the shade was almost pleasant. Almost. But for the excruciating thirst and nerve-wracking tension.

"What time is it?"

"Eleven-fifty." It was the sixth time in an hour he had asked. And I knew what he was thinking, what if Dion didn't come, and Willy stayed.

"Christ, I'm thirsty."

"You shouldn't have talked so much."

"I wanted you to know."

"I think I may have some peppermints. Look in my purse."

Mackin sucked his breath in noisily. "Jesus, that eye." He had found my compact and was studying himself in the mirror.

I smiled. "Your fans will love it."

He brought his eyes up, looked at me curiously, shrugged, then stuck his hand back in my purse. I put my head down on my hands and closed my eyes.

"Good Lord," he exclaimed. "Hertz, Avis, American Express, Air Travel . . . seven, eight, ten . . . are you kidding?"

Monday, I said wryly, "wants us to be prepared for any emergency."

"And lookee here, folks. A genuine laminated press card." He tapped my head. "Do you like working for *Monday,* Lindsie?"

I sighed and looked up. "Only when I get to poke into people's personal lives."

"But not when you have to write about football?"

"Football players," I corrected.

Mackin frowned at my card case. "Jesus, your father," he

said sourly. "It sure will be fun playing the Bears again. He'll have my head."

"I think it's your arm he wants. Said he'd trade his offensive line for you."

Mackin made a face. "I'm afraid he'll find me pretty offensive all right."

"Not Dad," I said with conviction. "Any man who names his only daughter after Lindsay Greenwood . . ."

Mackin grinned. "Yeah, I noticed the resemblance last night the way you tackled me."

"It's five after twelve."

He dropped my card case back into the purse and we crawled out of our cover and stood up. Presently, we heard the soft drone of an engine off to the right across the desert.

"Do you think they'll come looking for us?" said Mackin.

"I don't know." I didn't like our chances if they did.

The engine grew louder and for a scant few minutes we could see the plane dropping as it approached the far cluster of mountains. Just before it touched down, it disappeared behind them. The engine died. The desert grew still.

We waited.

"Here they come," Mackin whispered in my ear.

We had returned to our hiding place beneath the branches, lying flat on our stomachs head to head. Not moving, scarcely breathing. I could feel my heart pounding.

"How many?"

"Just Willy. No, wait. Dion and one other guy. The pilot."

I shut my eyes tight, an instinctive reflex, as if by my not seeing them they couldn't possibly be there. How long would they search? How high would they climb?

"Where are they now?" I whispered.

"Back a ways and below us. Willy has the damn gun."

I ventured a peek. Through the thicket of branches I could see them searching the low brush. Their voices drifted up to us.

"I'm sure they've gone," grumbled Willy impatiently.

"No," said Dion. "They've got to be here or in the valley. Otherwise you would have run into them last night."

"But they could have taken off across the desert by now," came Willy's protesting reply. "I think we ought to go out there." He was like a hungry retriever straining at the leash, his nose quivering for the smell of blood.

"If they did," said Dion calmly, "we'll spot them from the plane. But I have a feeling they're here."

Abruptly, he looked up, his eyes climbing the side of the mountain. He stood there, hands on hips, squinting against the glare. And then he was looking straight at me. My heart stopped.

"Willy," he yelled, his eyes still fixed in our direction, "you keep looking down here. George, you wander ahead and check the brush over there. I'm going up."

Was that a decoy to make us think he hadn't seen us? I could feel Mackin gripping my wrist.

"We'll take him if he comes up here," he breathed into my ear.

We waited interminably. I could hear the sound of Dion's shoes as he began climbing. He was still well behind us. I closed my eyes again, could feel the knots in my stomach, the pounding in my chest. Presently, the footsteps subsided. Mackin's painful grip on my wrist lessened and I could sense him raising his head.

"He's going the other way," he whispered.

Again the footsteps, but now, not as loud. I began to breathe again. Opened my eyes. I could see Willy poking at the brush down below. Sweat poured off my face and into my eyes.

Mackin squeezed my arm again. "He's coming back."

We waited. The footsteps grew louder. Then a new sound and my blood turned to ice.

"All right, you two, you can come out."

Mackin stiffened.

"Come on, Alex. We've got the money. You can be in San Diego in two hours."

The voice was so close that I feared if I opened my eyes I would find Dion standing right in front of me.

"You'll be a hero, Mackin. Don't be a fool."

Willy and the pilot had stopped searching and were staring fixedly at a point behind me. Mackin squeezed my wrist harder.

"We'll go down and wait for you in the jeep, Alex. We'll wait ten minutes. If you come down we won't hurt you and we won't go looking for the girl."

A pause. The tension was unbearable. But seemingly, Dion was only bluffing. He hadn't spotted us . . . yet.

"If you don't come down, Mackin, we'll get you on the way out and we'll kill you both."

I shuddered inwardly at the cold, matter-of-fact tone. Shuddered again knowing with a sickening finality that he was right.

"Ten minutes," he shouted. "It's your only chance."

I could hear him crunching and sliding back down the mountain. He called for Willy and George and I watched them in rising alarm as they marched out of sight, round the side of the mountain. The desert grew still once again, but for the insistent ticking of my watch.

I raised my head and looked at Mackin. His eyes were empty, his hands clenched; the barrier was fixed firmly between us. But then, our only link had been the desert and now he needn't be threatened by it anymore.

"Dion's right," I said hoarsely.

He dropped his eyes and I knew with rising resentment that he was debating.

"It's your only chance."

"I can't." The words held bitterness and once again we were strangers, linked by only one common bond: hate. He hated me for presenting him with a moral dilemma. And I hated him for having the choice. It was as basic as that.

"Self-preservation," I said quietly, "is no sin."

"No."

I didn't know if he were agreeing or disagreeing. "Alex," I said, "we'll both never make it. We'll both die."

He shook his head and said nothing.

"Go," I said again.

Mackin brought his eyes up to mine. "I can't," he whispered. "Don't you see? I couldn't bear being alone."

I saw then his predicament. He would be alone, too. Cut off from every other human being by the one awful memory he would always carry with him. He had to stay with me, not for my sake, but for his own. And suddenly I felt sorry for him. That it should come to this. I saw then too another Mackin. Without realizing it, I had gone into the interview with suspicion. Suspicion for all that success. And now I could see he had been holding that very same mistrust. When do you pay up? he had said, when, to me, he could have said anything to justify his lie. And he had chosen that.

"I understand," I whispered. And wished I could say more.

... Two rats. Two dirty, stinking desert rats inching across an endless expanse of pure white sand. Nomads, tired and miserable, plodding along. Burning rays of the sun pounding on our heads. Heat from the sand rising, suffocating. Dust and perspiration stiffening our clothes . . . desert rats. Making tiny tracks across a stark and empty moonscape.

Lindsie, don't you think, er, that this is, uh, well, a little melodramatic?

No, sir. It was a moonscape. The dictionary, it says in the dictionary . . .

But the rats?

Yes, sir, rats. Not humans. Burrowing into the sand . . .

"Lindsie, get up."

"I don't want to."

"You must. Come. Please come."

Mackin was talking again.

I wished he'd be quiet. I didn't want to listen to that harsh, cracked voice. It was like trying to fall asleep in a motel room and hearing the TV through the wall. I wanted to pound on him to shut up. But somehow, he was always . . . just out of reach.

". . . It forced me to grow up, you know? I even began to have doubts about football. Thought about quitting. But couldn't. All my life I'd wanted to be the greatest quarterback ever and

I couldn't just walk away from it not knowing. Now, I don't know. I tell myself it doesn't matter if I'm the best or not. Just the best I can be. But I haven't really come to grips with it yet because I still get pissed when people say I don't stack against Unitas or a passer like Jurgensen.

"I . . . isn't there a way to drink cactus? Didn't they teach you that? Oh, Lord . . . So I made a decision that had more to do with that winning season than the Super Bowl. And that was to keep a place for myself where I could get away from everybody and do my own thinking and find out who I was. It's like being eaten alive with all those people. It's scary, Lindsie, and it's . . . I don't know, humiliating, too, because they don't see you for yourself, but as some kind of status object. And after a while you begin despising yourself.

"So what I decided was this. I would be just what they wanted during the season because it seemed easier that way. And I have to admit, there are times when I enjoy the fuss, who wouldn't?

"But after the season, that's it. I just drop out. Last year I went to Africa for awhile. Once year I tried working with ghetto kids, but that was kind of a downer. Most of the time I just like to be out at sea. It's a strange life I guess, but it's the only way I know how to cope."

He fell silent then and it was like a steam drill shutting down, leaving only the blessed silence. The moment of dizziness had passed but I didn't know when it might hit again. Two o'clock. We had been walking since two, shortly after they had gone away. We had continued lying there, watching the small twin-engine vulture making lazy circles above the desert. Endless circles, round and round, rising and falling. And then it was gone, and a while later we had spotted the jeep crawling reluctantly back toward Kino Bay. And we had slid down from our perch and set off at an angle away from the Gulf, away from where they might expect us to be. Because I hadn't much hope they would give up so easily.

Again we stopped. The warm coarse cloth of the canteen, the even warmer metallic-tasting water. I took another drink, felt the tug, the canteen slipping through my fingers. And I hated him. Couldn't look at him, making me give up the water. White wavy footprints, glare, burned eyes, and the steam drill again. "It's funny they haven't come back."

I said nothing.

"Maybe they'll be waiting for us when we reach the brush. Somewhere along the road." A pause. "Suppose we don't circle back to the road? Suppose we go straight and cut through the brush? It'll be dark by then and they'll never find us in there."

"I don't think," I said at last, "we can get through the brush. We'll have to go along the road."

The small scuffing noises of the desert rats, regular, rhythmic . . . like the ticking of a clock. Stopping more often now and talking not at all. I was grateful for his silence as I trudged along beside him, his eyes downcast, his mouth firmly set. The mind had shut down. All the energy fueling the body, wondering how long until it finally broke down.

Six thirty. The watch said. Though who could tell? But, yes. Off to the right the sun was hovering just above the water, you could see the reflection, and it was cooler now. The first faint night breezes ruffling the sand. I collapsed on the ground and stared futilely at the brush, now a smudgy blur in the distance.

Mackin dropped down beside me and pulled off his shoes and socks. He began probing a half-dollar sized blister on the ball of his foot. I gently peeled off my own shoes and sat there massaging my feet. But I knew it wasn't going to do any good. We weren't going to make it. I was beginning to slide over the edge again. And I didn't care.

We ate in silence, the soft gooey chocolate coating our mouths like wet mud, refusing to go down sandpaper throats. We sipped a little water, not much left now, and tried to scrape the chocolate off the roofs of our mouths with swollen tongues. Soon the breathing would become difficult and there would be that strange tingling sensation in the arms and legs. Headaches, indistinct speech, skin a bluish color. Vision would dim. I had learned all about death from dehydration in Colorado.

I picked the foil off my last peppermint, broke it in two, reached out to Mackin. Nothing. He was sitting cross-legged staring gloomily off into the distance.

"What." A flat statement, not caring really.

"Thinking."

"What?" I said. Questioning now.

"That maybe we ought to stay here."

"No." Automatic response. Something in his tone.

He turned to me with glazed eyes. A whisper. "Then you go."

Something inside me began to knot up. "No," I said again. "We have to keep going." The flatness was gone. Was that panic in my voice?

"Go where, Lindsie? I bet we're not even halfway. And then what? They'll get us. Or even if they don't, do you have any idea how far it is to Kino? We'll never make it and you're crazy if you think we will."

I felt a sudden inward chill. Hadn't expected this from him. Hadn't given him so much as a thought as we had been walking. I had just assumed he was doing okay. But something had happened to him somewhere back across the miles. The slight shift in balance.

"No," I pleaded. "We're more than halfway. The worst is behind us. It's cooling off and once we reach the brush we can stop for the night and set up the water still. Don't you see? Another few hours and we'll be okay."

A lie. I had no idea how long it would take to reach the brush, no idea how dehydrated we were. But I was suddenly aware of a curious psychology at work. When he was strong, I let down, depending on him to see us through. But now he was slipping and the equilibrium had shifted. We were two people on a seesaw, and I had to get him back up.

"Let's go."

"No."

"All right."

Idly I began to trace a pattern in the sand. Four lines, no reason really, shaped like a rectangle. Another line to bisect, an X here, an O there. I glanced up and saw that he was watching.

"Silly, isn't it?" I said. "Pretending like it's third and long, with you right here—" I made another X. "But I was just thinking how remarkably cool you can be. The way you drop back and just wait . . . usually about here. Like you know it will all work out." I erased the lines and looked at him.

"But this is different, isn't it, Alex? Something hard and tough and you can't crack it. Out there you're in charge and there's the team, but now you have no team, and alone, you're nothing."

He had turned away. His gaze had fallen into his lap, the wind touching his hair, the way I wanted to touch him and couldn't. Softly I said, "It'll be okay, Alex. The sun will go down and you'll go to sleep and maybe you'll think something nice. Like that day you rolled out and ran it across the goal line with ten seconds and they lifted you up and carried you off the field. Because sometime in the night you'll slip away and when the sun is up and the vultures circle round you won't even . . ."

The dull green eyes drew sharply into focus and something began to change in his face. The mouth twitched, the flash of teeth, a dimple. "Screw you."

And so we set off again. And this time I made sure he talked.

For six years Mackin had heard nothing from Royce Dion, the man he now assumed was in the limousine. Then one Monday, in late November, he received a phone call at home.

"This is your friend from Vegas," the caller had said.

"I don't have any friends in Vegas," Mackin replied.

"Then let's just say this is your old business buddy."

Mackin froze.

"I've got another business venture to discuss with you, Mr. Mackin. Will tonight be all right?"

"Forget it," Mackin had said and hung up.

But that night Sam and Willy showed up at Mackin's apartment. They told him they were interested in insuring a point spread for the Super Bowl.

"Sam did all the talking. Said there was more money in it for me this time. I told him I wasn't interested. He said maybe I'd like to think about it. I said nothing to think about. Oh, yes, there is, he said. Said if I didn't cooperate he would make sure the commissioner found out about the other game. I said he already looked into it and found me clean. Drops a bombshell. Says when he brought me the money there was another guy outside with a camera. Got pictures of me taking the package and then came up to window and took some of me counting. I said he was bluffing. Two days later I get the snapshots in the mail. That night Sam calls. I said I'd think about it. Didn't know what the hell to do. Because nobody would believe me. And you see, in a way I *was* guilty. Just *thinking* about a fix makes you guilty. And I'd sat out the quarter and maybe even . . . stopped us from getting another score. Christ, is that water I hear? Oh, God . . .

"Uh, okay, following Monday they come again. Wanted my answer. I said okay. Figured no way you could insure a spread for sure, so I would just pretend to go along. Then if they hassled me after the game, I'd take my chances with the commissioner.

"But after they left I started thinking. This could go on forever. Anytime they wanted a fix, just call up ole Alex. I didn't know why they hadn't called me before, but I couldn't count on them waiting so long again.

". . . Realized I had only one choice. To quit. Even if I went to the commissioner it would create a stink. Kept thinking about my dad and how he wanted so much for me and how proud he was and I knew it would kill him if it ever got out about the fix, it really would.

"I, scuse me . . . uh, wasn't going to announce it until after the season. But one day I was talking to Hampton in the dressing room. He was really down 'cause he felt he had talent and it was being wasted. No chance to play unless I got injured. So somehow I let it slip I wouldn't be around next year and some reporter . . . Christ, I hope my knee's going to be okay. It's awfully *shaky*.

"So a couple of days later I get a call from Sam, in the dressing room for chrissake, saying what the hell is this all about? And I say, pipe down, buddy, the guy misquoted me. Happens all the time. And he says if I think I can wiggle out of it by threatening to retire, they'd spill the story to all the papers *before* the Super Bowl and try to get me suspended, if not the whole team. So I say, not to worry, everything's cool and I didn't hear from them again until the night you came. Guess they were just waiting to make sure we were going to the Super Bowl."

Mackin didn't say anything for a long time. The moon had risen and was casting its queer shadows on the desert. Cardone and seguro cactus loomed eerily before us as we trudged on, walking mechanically now, too exhausted to feel the pain.

"Time's it?" A rasp. His voice nearly gone.

"Almost nine. Almost there."

We had begun angling right, back toward the Gulf and the sandy road that led into Kino Bay. While he had been talking,

I had decided we ought to cut all the way over and approach the road from the right instead of the left, as they might expect. Then instead of ducking in and out of the brush beside the road, we could walk by the water. It would be the longer route, but by night, the safest. Or so I thought.

"What happened then?" I said.

He shook his head. "Can't talk anymore."

We poked along until nearly midnight. My legs felt like they were dragging bowling balls, but worse, I was experiencing dizzy spells and frightening bouts of double vision. And then something new, a roaring in my ears. I began to panic.

"Oh, God," said Mackin suddenly.

I stopped and followed his eyes. Then the wind picked up and with it the wonderfully pungent smell of ocean salt. The roaring of course. I sighed and closed my eyes, knowing we'd be okay now. But when I opened them, Mackin was gone.

He had been standing just behind me. This is crazy, I thought. "Alex?"

And then I spotted him, down near the water. With relief I started toward him. Stopped cold. He had thrown the canteen down and was marching determinedly toward the water.

I stumbled after him and grabbed his arm. "Don't be ridiculous," I said. "It will kill you."

"Leggo." He jerked his arm away.

"Be quiet," I urged desperately. "Alex . . ."

He was knee-deep in water and bending over. I scrambled after him, grabbed his arm again, and tried to pull him back. He yanked free, staggering and falling into the water. I sloshed over to him, got hold of his arm and began tugging . . . futilely.

"You mustn't swallow the water," I said.

"Hell with you. Leggo."

I had both hands on his wrist. Was tugging, when forcefully, he jerked back his arm and I flew off into the water. Got up and found Mackin scooping water in his mouth. Lunged on top of him and we both tumbled backward. Staggered to my feet, found him standing above me with his fist raised. I ducked. Rose slowly, turned to face him. He drew his arm back again. I lowered my head and went for his stomach. Knocked him back into the water. He started to get up and I threw water in his face. He sputtered. In desperation, I pulled off a shoe, splashed around behind him, and brought it crashing down on his head. He grunted and slumped forward. I grabbed him under the arms to keep his head above water, and saw that I hadn't knocked him out, just stunned him.

When he started moaning, I said, "In ten seconds I'm going to let go of you, walk onto the beach, pick up the canteen and take off. If you want to stay here and drink up the whole blasted Gulf, do it. I can't stop you. Do you understand that?"

Imperceptibly, he nodded. I let go of him and stepped back. When he didn't fall over, I turned and walked to shore. Pulled off my other shoe and stood there shivering. My clothes were soaked through and I could feel the sharp sting of salt in my mouth. I was so furious with him that I didn't honestly care what he did. But a moment later, he rose unsteadily and stumbled out of the water. He looked at me with great soulful eyes.

"I'm sorry, Lindsie."

I was too angry to speak. I found the canteen, twisted off the cap and took a bare sip of water, swirling it around my mouth and spitting it out. I gave the rest to Mackin.

"Try to get the salt out of your mouth. Take a small sip, then spit it out."

He did what I said.

"Now drink the rest of it and let's go."

He stood there looking at me sorrowfully.

"Come on, Alex. It will dilute the salt water in your stomach."

"I'm really sorry, Lindsie."

I smiled. "I know."

We started walking along the narrow strip of beach, the wet sand felt good against my feet. After a while the land began sloping up and the beach opened on a shallow cove. Somewhere above us lay the sandy road, and although I knew from the ride out, it would begin veering inland, I didn't know where. The wind blew cold off the Gulf and the water temperature was actually warmer than the air. My teeth chattered like castanets.

"How's your head?"

"Awful." Then, "Lindsie? I think I'm going to be sick."

"It's the salt water," I said.

Suddenly he bent over, and began heaving. A thin trickle of water ran from his mouth.

"Can't go on," he moaned.

I was too exhausted to fight him anymore. Had to think. Had to get my brain out of stall. I walked away from Mackin, dug a cigarette unthinkingly from my purse, cupped my hand around the lighter and inhaled. Two choices. One: I go on without him, try to reach Kino before ten when the sun would drive me blindly into the sea. Or two: Stay with Mackin, try to rub the salt off his jacket and hope to condense enough water to see us through another day.

Stood there, debating, smoking, shivering. Made the decision. Dropped the cigarette, walked back to Mackin and squatted down beside him.

"I'm going on without you," I said.

"Lindsie, you can't leave me."

"I'm going to try to get to Kino, Alex. I'll get help and come back for you."

His teeth were chattering so fiercely that his whole body shook. "No, please," he whispered.

"What we'll do," I went on, "is walk up to the road and cross it and find you a place to wait. You'll be able to fall asleep and pretty soon I'll be back."

"What if something happens to you?"

"It won't."

"But what if it does?" he demanded. "Do you want to die alone?"

"No."

We were both shaking so badly we could hardly get the words out. "Let's at least go up to the road," I suggested, "and get out of the wind."

We began climbing the sandy incline. I was carrying my shoes in one hand and trying to support Mackin with the other. His legs kept buckling under him and it took all my strength to keep us both from tumbling over. Eventually we reached the top and I found we hadn't come far at all. The sandy road was still right there.

"I'm burning up," said Mackin hoarsely.

I touched his cheek. Burning up indeed. His eyes were glazed and he was shaking from head to foot. I glanced desperately around, half looking for a place he could collapse—and half looking for Crazy Willy. My eyes stopped. Down the beach, well beyond the cove, came a faint glimmer.

"Let's walk a little," I urged.

I put an arm around his waist and we began moving slowly along the road. The glimmer, which I feared might merely be a reflection on the water, grew brighter.

"It looks like a campfire," I said. "Why don't you stay here and I'll go see."

"What if it's them?" said Mackin.

"Then at least we'll know where they are."

I got him across the road and settled in the brush. Dropped my shoes and purse.

Then I set off down the road.

A jeep was parked by the road.

I crept up to it cautiously. No one inside. No keys in the ignition. A dark wool jacket lay on the driver's seat. I reached in through the open window and drew it out. The pockets were empty. I put it on and peered over the embankment. Below, on the beach, two men were sitting cross-legged by the fire with their backs to me. Two men and, counting them, twelve sleeping bags, and a tent.

I picked up a rock and sent it cascading down the incline. The larger of the two men turned, rose slowly to his feet, and looked up the hill.

It was the fitful moaning that pulled me awake. I drifted to my senses only to find I couldn't move. My legs seemed to have weights on them. My arms were pinned to my sides. And I was thirsty. Unbearably thirsty.

Mackin groaned again. I worked my arms out of the blanket and pulled his head onto my chest. I stroked his damp cheek and whispered his name. With a start, he opened his eyes and began thrashing about. His elbow crashed against my face.

"Alex, be still."

"Lindsie?"

"It's all right, lie down."

"Where are we?"

His voice was no more than a whisper. Granules of salt

dotted his mustache. He looked at me with bright, feverish eyes.

"In the tent. How are you feeling?"

"Thirsty."

"I'll get some water."

"I'm dying."

"Then you must be feeling better."

He made a face and snuggled closer. "I dreamed I was dying," he said as if this were indisputable proof.

"Really?"

"Yes. I was crawling in the desert. No water. And I had to get to the game. I was late, you see, and they would fine me and I kept crawling faster and my leg fell off. I picked it up and hung it around my neck 'cause I figured the trainer could glue it back on. But then . . ."

"Alex," I said, trying not to laugh, "we're okay now."

"No," he said positively. "They can still get me."

I kissed the top of his head. "Not any more."

The sun glancing off the water nearly blinded me as I crawled out of the tent, wrapped mummylike in the blanket. Twelve scruffy, unshaven men, sitting in a circle on the beach, put down twelve tin plates and stared at me in wide-eyed unison.

Stretch Wilson, the Outward Bound instructor I had met in Kino, stood and hurried over. Being the instructor, I noticed, had its advantages. Under the cowboy hat, his face was clean-shaven.

"How is he?" He looked at me with concern. "How are *you?*"

"I think he may have a fever. My only problem is hundred-year-old legs."

Stretch grinned. He had a piece of egg stuck between his two front teeth. "I've got some aspirin," he drawled. "And I'll get your clothes and bring y'all some breakfast. Powdered eggs Benedict this morning."

"Thank you."

"Sure," he said easily. I could see the amusement in his eyes.

After getting Mackin to bed, I had told Stretch about the kidnapping. He had graciously offered us his tent, but I had the distinct feeling he thought I was sun-crazed.

"What did you tell them?" I said, noticing all those eyes still gaping.

"Just that you and your friend got lost. But it's been some time since they've seen a woman."

"I guess this will cure them for a while," I said laughing.

"You kidding? After seventeen days in the desert you look like Raquel Welch to them."

Raquel must not be doing so good, I thought, as Stretch went to fetch our clothes. He had laid them out on gear packs beside the fire so by now they were dry, and stiff as cardboard.

I crawled back into the tent and tossed Mackin his jeans and shirt.

"Can you get dressed?" I said.

An emphatic shake of the head. "I'm too sick. Nearly dead." This was stated with absolute certainty.

"Do you know," I said, "that as a group, athletes are the biggest physical cowards after doctors?"

"That's 'cause we know the fraility of the human condition."

"Mm." I stepped into my slacks.

"Do you know," said Mackin sitting up, "that you've got a fantastic body?"

I reached for my shirt. "Like Raquel Welch's?"

Mackin grimaced. "Remind me to tell you about her some-time."

"How much time do I have?"

"What?"

"Before you die."

Six hours in the back of a flatbed truck wasn't my idea of fun. But the only flight from Hermosillo to Tijuana had already left, and though we could have made the one to Tucson, I couldn't think of a more likely place than the airport for them to be waiting.

Outdoorsman Stretch Wilson was no football fan, saying even if he fell over Alex Mackin he wouldn't recognize him, but at last he gave in and agreed to drive his slightly mad country-men to San Diego. We had chosen the truck over his jeep so we could watch the road for Willy and duck under the blankets if we spotted him. Which further confirmed Stretch's wary opinion of us.

In the odd moments when Mackin wasn't (a) dying, (b) sure he was going to throw up, (c) tending to his shoulder or knee, he talked of how Dion and Sam set out to blackmail him. I found an old magazine in the back of the truck and made notes in the margin.

"They should have seen that that was the thing to do," said Mackin. "Have a couple of drinks and wait you out. But no, they had to go and drug you. Dion was furious. Cause otherwise you would never have suspected. But it was an amazingly sloppy operation all along. You'd think with that kind of money on the line, they'd be smoother.

"Anyway, after you passed out they took me to Dion's con-dominium. Then they drugged *me* with 100 cc's of amobarbital, a needle in the arm and I'm out cold till late the next morning when Dion himself arrives. He tells me the Chargers are five-point favorites to win the Super Bowl, so naturally they want to bet on St. Louis. With me in their pocket they could double their money.

"I tell him there's no way I'm going to dump the game. He starts talking money. I can see he isn't going to give up. Quarter of a million, he says again. I pretend to consider, finally agree.

" 'Good,' he says. 'Now if you'll just sign this.'

"Well, goddamn, if it isn't a piece of paper that says I,

Alexander Mackin, promise to the best of my ability to insure that the San Diego Chargers lose the Super Bowl game to St. Louis. All typed up like a fucking legal document.

" 'You're out of your mind,' I tell him.

" 'It's our insurance,' he says. 'If you balk, this paper goes to the commissioner. With your signature on it.'

"I argue. I say there's no way I can insure it. And there isn't. Hell, some of my passes are gonna have to connect. I can't go oh-for-thirty. And I can't stop my backs. And I can't stop my defense. And what if Richards runs back a punt? He says sign it. I say no. Okay, he says, the photographs go to the commissioner.

"I tell him I need to think about it. He leaves. They tie me up and shoot me with a little more amobarbital, not enough to knock me out but just enough to keep me groggy. That night, another full dose. Next day, back comes Dion. He says we're going to my apartment. What for, I ask. To call Crittenden, he says, and wish him a Happy New Year. Well, this doesn't make sense to me, but I figure anything's better than signing my name to that paper. I hope you're getting this straight 'cause I'm probably going to die. Jesus! Where does he think he is, Indy?"

Mackin started coughing again. I offered him the canteen Stretch had provided and lit a cigarette for myself. No cars following us. "That was to set up the kidnapping then?"

"I guess. Although I think they were still hoping to get their money back through the game. Anyway, I called Crittenden and said I was in the mountains and everything was fine. Then we go back to the condominium. By that time I had decided I would try to keep stalling them until I could escape. I figured I would take my chances with the commissioner. Maybe we could work out a deal where he would hush it up and I would retire. But I never had the opportunity because they kept me doped. That day and the next two days, and every day Dion comes with more threats. Finally it's Friday and they know I'm supposed to be in New Orleans. Dion says this is my last chance. I still told him no."

We were pulling into a gas station and a frail old man rose slowly out of his chair. "So how did they get you into Mexico then?" I asked.

"I think they had phony tourist cards," said Mackin.

Phony tourist cards and yet Dion had used his own plane and rented a car under his own name. Interesting.

"She's lying," screamed Crittenden for the umpteenth time. "Any idiot can see that."

We were all in Mackin's living room. Sgt. Quaid on the couch with his notebook and me. Detective Leon standing by the window. An FBI agent and Crittenden in the leather chairs. And a police stenographer perched on the coffee table scribbling madly. The head physician for the Los Angeles Rams, who had followed calmly in Crittenden's stormy wake, was in the bedroom—where Mackin, predictably, was dying again.

"She was in cahoots with them," said Crittenden furiously. "I know it, dammit. Otherwise, why did she break into my office?"

"To steal your game film and ransom it back to you?" I suggested.

"Lindsie," said Quaid evenly, "why were you so interested in that particular film?"

We'd been at it for over an hour. I had been through my story, and two pints of orange juice, and Crittenden hadn't liked any of it. With good reason. I'd neglected to mention the fix in that other Super Bowl game and it left a couple of gaping holes. I had neglected to mention it because one, it wasn't a matter for the San Diego police since it had happened in Miami. And two, I knew now Crittenden had no inkling of it and I wasn't about to tell him. Besides, coming from me, he would have erupted like a volcano and ruined Mackin's jungle decor.

"Because," I said carefully, "when I was interviewing Alex's roommate, he mentioned that particular game. And I wanted to include the highlights of Mackin's career in my story."

Quaid started doodling. The police stenographer flipped a page of his notebook. The FBI agent looked haggard.

"What I can't understand," said Quaid, shifting to one of the gaping holes, "is why, if the kidnappers approached Mackin a month ago, he didn't report it."

I said it beat me.

Quaid sighed heavily. "All right, we'll get that from Mackin tomorrow. Now," he said more hopefully, "I want an accurate description of this man called Dion."

I gave him one.

Quaid asked Leon for the picture. He handed it to me. "Is this the man, Lindsie?"

I glanced at the glossy. Wide cheekbones, a small nose, rimless glasses, but in the photograph he looked older, tougher, somehow more villainous than the bland, pale man in the desert. "No," I said to Quaid, "not quite. Dion's face is thinner and his mouth is different. Unless maybe this is a very old picture."

The doctor emerged from the bedroom. He was a tall, kindly looking man with white hair and ruddy cheeks. And a deep, gruff voice. "I've checked him over, Harley, and I've given him a mild sedative. The man is exhausted. He was severely dehydrated and he's running a slight fever. I've instructed him to drink a pint of liquid every hour and to eat soup and milkshakes until the mucuous linings of his mouth are healed. He's got a few bruises but otherwise he's fine."

Crittenden frowned. "Well?" he demanded. "Will my quarterback be able to play or not?"

Poor Alex, I thought.

The doctor considered. "Today is Wednesday. My advice would be to have him stay home and rest, maybe catch a noon flight Friday. A mild workout that afternoon, Harley, no more than forty-five minutes. No scheduled practice after that, right? Have Sims get a couple of receivers to work out with Alex on Saturday. How long he'll be able to go on Sunday, if at all, I can't say. By the way," he added turning to me, "Alex wants to see you. But please, just for a minute."

I entered the darkened bedroom and sat on the edge of the bed. He was lying on his back, his head propped up on two pillows, the bleeding-heart sheet pulled up to his chin.

I smiled. "Bad news, huh?"

"What do you mean?" he whispered hoarsely.

"Doctor says you'll live."

Mackin nodded absently. "I suppose. Uh, Lindsie? I was wondering just what you told them."

"Everything."

He looked at me in alarm. "Everything I told you?"

"Well, I probably forgot a few things."

"What about the game?" he said impatiently.

"I told them Dion wanted you to dump it. And you refused."

"No, no. I mean the other game?"

"Sometimes," I said, "you tell reporters stories."

Mackin looked surprised, then hopeful. "And you're not going to write about it either?"

The obvious question he would ask. And I couldn't tell him the answer. I wanted to reach out and touch him. Wanted to crawl under the awful sheet and curl up in his arms and feel that warm gorgeous body. And all I could do was say, "Alex, I don't know yet."

"Why not?" He paused and I could see the answer forming in his mind. "Oh," he said. "Of course. You didn't tell the police because they'd tell the press and you'd lose your big scoop. Well congratulations, Lindsie. I hope you enjoy the publicity."

Oh, God.

Back to square one. He was once again the football player with a reputation to protect, and I was the reporter with a story to write. Ambitious, distrustful, and selfish.

I said, "It's just that I have to think it all out. Believe me, if there's no point, I won't write it."

"Point?" he snapped. "What point? To sensationalize the story?" His eyes flashed angrily.

"No," I said softly. "I wouldn't do that. That's just as bad as covering up something that should be made known."

"And this should?"

I shifted uncomfortably and waited for Mackin to go on. But he didn't say anything and gradually the anger went out of his eyes.

"Okay," he said quietly.

I started to get up.

"Lindsie?"

"Yes."

"I just want you to know that whatever happens, I'll always be grateful to you for getting me out of the desert."

"I think it was the other way around."

He smiled faintly. "Take care, Lindsie."

"See you, Alex."

I closed the door behind me and didn't suppose I ever would.

I made a quick call to Maxwell to let him know I was okay and on the way home. Sgt. Quaid offered to drive me to Brown Field to pick up my rental car. Leon stayed behind to take the first shift of an around-the-clock watch on Mackin. The doctor volunteered to fetch some groceries for Alex, after persuading Crittenden not to disturb him until the next day.

As Quaid turned off La Jolla onto Garnet, I asked how he had traced us to Hermosillo. I had overheard him asking the FBI agent if there had been any word on Willy from the men down there.

"The night we visited you at the hotel," he said, "you gave us our first real lead. You mentioned Dion. We got hold of his secretary and she said he was in Mexico on business and had been for eight days, and she didn't see how he could have been in San Diego. She said she didn't know how to reach him, that he always called in. I asked if she had booked his flight. She said he always made his own arrangements.

"Sunday, I had people check the airports in Las Vegas and San Diego and we finally traced him to Mexico City."

"Mexico City?" I said.

"Yeah. He had flown a commercial flight from Vegas to Mexico City on December twenty-ninth. The FBI went down to look for him."

Quaid turned onto U.S. 5 South and grumbled at a small truck that wouldn't move over for him.

"On Monday," he continued, "two things happened. First, we get a call that a car had been left overnight at Brown Field and something about a woman going to Hermosillo and not returning. Had someone check and discovered, of course, it was you. I sent a man down there and in the course of going through the car rental forms, not only does he find yours, but Dion's. Interesting, huh? My man also learned that Dion's private plane had been there since Saturday night and had left within the hour, presumably for San Diego. But the plane never landed here, at least not at any of the airports.

"Then around six, Crittenden gets another call. We tried to trace it but it was just under two minutes and we couldn't get a fix on it. The caller told Crittenden to drive alone to a deserted airstrip east of the city at ten o'clock that night. There would

be a plane there. He was to walk up to the passenger window
and place the money on the seat. Mackin would be on the plane.
As soon as the money was on the plane, he would be released.
Sounded pretty damn foolproof because we couldn't follow
Crittenden all the way in. The airstrip was on high ground up
in the Laguana Mountains and the letter said specifically no
police or no Mackin. We did, however, have a couple of heli-
copters on standby ready to radio a pursuit plane."

I noticed Quaid turning off the freeway at the downtown exit.
I interrupted to remind him we were going to Brown Field.

"I know," he said. "But if you don't mind, I want to stop off
at headquarters first. Anyway, the strange thing is that Crittenden went out there but the plane never showed. He drove back
home thinking he had misunderstood his instructions. But we
never heard from them again."

"What? But Dion said he had the money."

Quaid turned and looked at me sideways. "Did he? That's
interesting."

He turned into the parking area fronting a stately Spanish-
style pink stucco building. Over the center archway were the
words City of San Diego Police Department.

"I guess," I said in confusion, "that all you have to do now
is find Dion."

Quaid switched off the engine.

"We already have."

Chapter 22

"You've made a mistake."

Quaid picked up the phone. My eyes drifted about the room. Powder blue walls, beige wall-to-wall carpeting, four groupings of desks, each group consisting of four desks pushed together to form a square. Most of the desks were vacant. The three teams of homicide detectives who had been working round the clock on the Mackin kidnapping had been sent home.

Quaid put down the receiver and turned back to me. His faded blue eyes held more color than before, brought out by the redness of his lower lids.

"That man," I said again, "is the man in the picture. He's not Royce Dion."

"Royce Dion," recited Quaid leaning back in his chair. "The man who developed Grand Pacifica Estates. The man who owns the Grand Nevada Hotel. The man with a missing Beechcraft Baron. Royce Francis Dion."

I shifted in my chair and noticed a schedule of Charger games tacked to the bulletin board. "Look," I said, "I know I was under stress. But that man is not the one I saw. His face is too wide. His nose is too flat. His voice is deeper. His glasses have no frames, whereas Dion's had metal ones."

Quaid looked at me for a long moment. "I don't suppose," he said, "that you'd like to tell me why you went to look at the game film."

"But I already did," I answered too quickly.

"No you didn't," he said quietly.

I looked at Quaid and said nothing.

A grunt. "Okay, so you're protecting Mackin. Or maybe he didn't mean to blow that pass at all. To be honest, I couldn't tell one way or the other from looking at the film."

"You looked at the film?"

"Of course. You threw out the name Dion, a known gambler. You were very insistent on seeing film from a game played six years ago, and not even a particularly memorable game at that. We thought you might be onto something."

"Oh."

Quaid opened his drawer. "Anyway, that's the NFL's problem because Miami won't touch it." He found a roll of Clorets and offered me one. "The penalty for illegal gambling in most places is only a few hundred bucks. Most police departments have better things to do."

"Okay. But what does this have to do with the man down the hall?"

"That man," said Quaid, "is being held for questioning. But we can only hold him thirty-six hours. He's due to be released in the morning unless we can find something to book him on. I don't think we can."

"I don't understand."

"No?" He leaned back and brought his feet up on the desk. "Look, Mackin was theoretically kidnapped early last Monday morning from his apartment, thirty-six hours *after* the real Royce Dion boarded a plane in Las Vegas for Mexico City. He was working on a deal to buy a hotel and we have him pretty well nailed down the whole time Mackin was being held. In short, we don't have a shred of evidence to pin on him."

"You mean," I said, "Dion arranged for his own imposter and you can't prove it?"

"How?"

"What about his plane?"

Quaid smiled sourly. "Stolen. We picked him up in Mexico City yesterday and before we could even read him his rights his office was on the phone reporting his plane's gone and damned if his condominium isn't broken into as well."

"But he must have set up the whole thing," I said.

"Sure. But according to Dion, Sam and his pilot were behind the operation. Convenient because one's dead and the other's missing. And the phony Dion, I suspect, will either leave the country for good. Or turn up dead."

I remembered then how Dion and Sam had laughed when Dion suggested having me killed in a plane crash. Presumably he would arrange it to look like he had been on board, too. Clever.

I said, "What about a lie detector test?"

Quaid made a face. "A waste of time, Lindsie. The D.A.'s office in Las Vegas is buried under Dion's test tapes. The man gets investigated the way you go to the dentist. And nobody's ever got to him yet."

I sighed. "Do you suppose I could have something to drink?"

"Oh, sorry. George! Will you get a couple cans of juice from the cafeteria?"

I said, "Sergeant, I still don't understand why the phony Dion didn't pick up the money."

"Excuse me, a bit warm in here, don't you think?" Quaid got up and opened two windows. I didn't think it was that warm.

He sat down and leaned way back in his chair. "Okay. Two possibilities. One, they suspected a trap. Or got scared. Or maybe got in touch with the real Dion in Mexico City and he called it off. Remember, he hadn't expected us to latch onto him. And we wouldn't have either if you hadn't mentioned his name. This whole elaborate ruse with the imposter was devised in the one in a hundred chance we did suspect him."

"It seems to me," I mused, "that if they'd gone to all that trouble to recover their bets they would have at least tried to get the ransom."

Quaid pinched the bridge of his nose and breathed in noisily. "Maybe," he said slowly. "But they could also have gone back down to Kino and broken the hell out of Mackin's arm and hoped it would be enough to keep the Chargers from winning. Then their bets would have been safe."

Perhaps, I thought, that was why they had told Mackin they had the money. To get him to come out so they could injure him. I said, "What's your second theory?"

Quaid gave me a small wintry smile. "That the kidnapping wasn't a kidnapping at all."

"I . . . what?"

Quaid leaned forward. "Listen," he said eagerly, "Mackin told you they wanted him to fix the Super Bowl game and he refused. So to get back the money they had already put down on the Cards they went to Crittenden for the ransom, right? Well suppose Mackin did not refuse. Suppose he agreed? Everything's all set. They take the Cards as underdogs, plunk down one million two, and wait for Mackin to dump the game. But then you turned up at his apartment that Sunday night. And they didn't know how much you knew or suspected. So . . . ."

"No," I interrupted. "They didn't know I was a reporter. Dion asked me whom I worked for."

Quaid grinned. "Come on, Lindsie, you're smarter than that. Mackin knew."

"All right." The juice arrived and I downed both cans lickety split. Soon I wouldn't need to fly home—I could float.

"So," said Quaid, "they switched gears and made it *look* like a kidnapping. That way when Mackin played badly in the game, there'd be a good reason for it."

"He might," I said wryly, "have eventually been asked by the police for descriptions of his kidnappers."

"And," added Quaid, "given phony ones. At least of Dion. As for Sam and Willy, they were expendable." He paused. "Sure is warm in here, excuse me."

A third window flew open and I suddenly realized Quaid's problem: Me. I moved my chair back a bit.

"You also," I pointed out, "seem to forget that Mackin killed Sam."

"And convinced you beyond a shadow of a doubt that he was an innocent victim."

I stared at Quaid in disbelief.

"Of course," he went on, "by that time he was probably pretty scared. He hadn't counted on you showing up."

"And I wouldn't have either if you had bothered to tell me a few things."

Quaid smiled. "The ransom call said no press. So we called your boss to find out if we could trust you. He said we couldn't."

"Is there anything else you'd like to tell me?" I said sardonically. "I mean Mackin mentioned something about a rape-murder . . ."

"Really?" He yawned. "I don't know, Lindsie. Maybe the guy is innocent. I'm just exploring possibilities."

"A bit far-fetched, aren't they?"

"Perhaps." A pause. "But let me try this out on you. Do you know what the line is these days on the Super Bowl? Chargers favored by three. And still the big money won't come in without points. Privately, word has been going around the Chargers can't win."

"Well that makes sense. Even if people still believe he has the flu . . ."

"No. Word got out Monday night after Dion's plane failed to show."

"Okay, so people understandably don't want to bet on the Chargers until they find out what kind of shape Mackin's in. So what?"

Quaid grinned. "So do you know what happened on Sunday?"

"The Super Bowl was kidnapped?"

"The Cards' big running back . . . what's his name?"

"Scooter Sherwood?"

"Yeah. Broke his ankle in practice. Sunday morning. Sunday night, when it was still believed Mackin had the flu but would be fine for the game, a couple million dollars came in on the Cards. Don't you think that's odd?"

I felt my stomach knot, and wondered if Mackin were duping me still.

"Lindsie," he said gently. "I've been a cop for twenty years and I bet I'm almost as cynical as you are. Plenty of times that cynicism works against me. But I'll tell you this. Come Sunday, this is one guy who's going to have his eyes glued to the TV set. You can bet on it."

Quaid dropped me off at Brown Field to retrieve my rental car. Filthy and smelly, I arrived at San Diego Airport, bought a ticket home, and scurried into the ladies' room. I scrubbed as best I could and dressed in a fresh set of clothes. I figured that would help.

Apparently, it didn't.

The man who sat next to me on the plane eventually got up. And never returned.

Showered, scrubbed, and sloshing with coffee, I appeared in Maxwell's office late the next morning. He greeted me with a rare display of warmth, going so far as to jump out of his chair and hurry across the Chinese rug to pump my arm. He invited me to join him on his leather couch where, over still more coffee, I told him the whole story, including Quaid's suspicions.

Maxwell puffed on his pipe and stared out across the room. At last he turned to me. "I have to go with you, Lindsie. What do you think?"

"You mean," I said with faint sarcasm, "you trust me?"

Maxwell grunted. "Don't be ridiculous. Of course I trust you."

"In that case," I said, "I think Quaid is just frustrated that he can't hang the kidnapping on Dion."

"And Mackin is innocent?"

"Yes, I think so."

"You think," Maxwell challenged, "or you hope?"

I chewed on my lip. "Well, I do hope," I said candidly. I smiled. "I mean I'd hate to think I went tearing off into the desert to rescue a crook."

Maxwell turned slightly green.

"Okay. But I also know that the man I met out there wouldn't dump the game. Thing is, is he the same man who plays football?" Chip had seemed to think he was.

"The man who plays football," Maxwell pointed out, "did consider fixing the other game."

"I know that. But that was a different man, too. A foolish, immature kid who let all that success go to his head. For a while. For one quarter. I honestly don't think he'd do it now. But . . ."

"But what?"

"Sir, I haven't told you everything. But in the desert, well, it was kind of rough, and the point is, if Mackin was able to lie so convincingly under those conditions, then he's not only a natural-born athlete, but a natural-born liar. And if that's the case, I doubt we'd ever be able to prove anything against him."

I began trying to chew off a piece of dead skin on my lip.

Maxwell chewed his pipe. A couple of cows deliberating over the morning cud. Only when he chewed, it was a sign that his computer-like mind was whirring away. I patiently awaited the output. His eyes would light up first.

His eyes lit up. "Okay. You go home and write the story. Make it first person. Tell about the kidnapping from beginning to end. But don't mention Mackin's being approached on that other game. We'll give him the benefit of the doubt. However . . ."

"What?"

"I want you to prepare an insert that describes in detail what happened six years ago. And be careful how you word it. Then . . ."

"Then I go to the Super Bowl, right? And when I call in the game stuff we make a decision?"

Maxwell, of course, was way ahead of me. He tapped my knee. "We do better than that. If the Chargers lose, we call Quaid. Get his opinion. If he thinks Mackin dumped it, we'll say someone close to the investigation suspects blah, blah, blah. That way we won't get hit with a libel suit from here to China. What do you think?"

"How many words?"

"Just write."

Chapter 23

Super Bowl Sunday dawned bright, sunny, and warm. I knew, for I had been awake to see it, dressed and fidgeting in my hotel room, waiting for this Event of Events to begin.

I arrived at the Louisiana Superdome early, making my way up the ramp to its underbelly, then rattling around its perimeter like a roulette ball in search of the press gate. A man in a snappy blue uniform checked my NFL press credentials the way a numismatist might examine a rare coin and waved me toward an elevator. Up on the Loge level, I found the working press area. It extended from the fifty-yard line down to about the thirty, with the main television booth on the other side of the fifty. My assigned seat was in the first row of the press box, five reporters down from the fifty. This, no doubt, a result of the kidnapping. Otherwise, I probably would have been stuck in the concessions stand. They still weren't too keen on women in the press box.

There were a few typewriters scattered about, but no other reporters. In the TV booth next door, anxious men checked clipboards and combed their hair. I shuffled through a three-inch stack of press releases that I found stuffed in a cheap leather zipper case on my chair, as commercials for beer and automobiles flashed across a six-sided screen suspended from the Dome roof, and the first of the 81,187 spectators began to arrive.

Eventually, I wandered across the corridor to the press lounge for a cup of coffee. There were tables and chairs, and counters groaning with food, but I never even got close. A zillion eyes swiveled my way and suddenly I had notebooks and microphones jammed under my nose. After a few dozen insipid questions, I wormed my way out and sat impatiently in my seat through all the pre-game crap.

The Chargers won the coin toss—"For this exciting Super Bowl we have obtained a 2,000-year-old Roman coin!" a press release said—and elected to receive. Their kick-return team took the field and ran the ball back to the twenty-eight. The Super Bowl was underway.

Mackin, with a big number 7 on his back, crouched down in the huddle and gave his instructions. The team lined up, Mackin took the snap, faked to his right, then he rifled a pass to his flanker for a 39-yard gain. There was a moment of stunned silence. Then a great cry went up in the Superdome. So much for Mackin's inability to throw.

Indeed. After Chip lunged through the middle for three more yards, Mackin was dropping back again. And he was perfect. The ball slammed into the hands of his tight end down near the Cardinals' sixteen.

This produced a mass groan. Holding against the Chargers.

Back went the ball to the forty. Still second down. Mackin called for the draw play and Chip scampered for seven yards. Third and ten. Another faked handoff and then Mackin sent the ball spinning out to his split end. Who caught it on the eighteen —just out of bounds. As Mackin jogged off the field, the fans gave him a noisy standing ovation.

The bulky reporter on my right squinted up at the scoreboard clock and typed: "Standing 0—Mack, 12:47."

The crowd was still on its feet as the field goal team trotted out. The kick was partially blocked and squirted into the end zone; the fans deflated back into their purple, green, and red seats.

Led by their stocky quarterback, Max Wiggins, the Cardinals

began their drive downfield. Slow and meticulous, Wiggins worked his team down to the Chargers' twenty-five on a third down. Whatever play he called next, he shouldn't have. His pocket collapsed, and so did Wiggins, and out came the field goal team.

Their kicker didn't miss. Three-nothing Cards.

A girl in a miniskirt came by gripping a cardboard box and asked if I wanted a sandwich. I did not. I was too busy watching Mackin. He was still depending on his arm, confusing the Cardinal defense, which had been sure that he would not.

First down on his own forty-three.

And Mackin wasn't through with his surprise yet. Chip took Mackin's handoff, then to the Cardinals' astonishment—and everyone else's—flipped the ball backward to Mackin, who threw a pass good for 36 yards. Just like that.

"I'll be dammed," muttered the reporter next to me. "That's Namath's old flea-flicker play."

First down on the twenty-one and Mackin was again drifting back, waiting for anyone to get clear in the end zone. But the opposing lineman was almost upon him. Hurriedly, Mackin threw into the crowd. The ball wound up in the arms of a blazing red Cardinal.

The minutes ticked away.

Still Mackin passed. It was clever strategy. But as the first quarter ended, it proved to be futile strategy. Something always went just a little awry.

But five minutes into the second quarter there was Mackin deep in Cardinal territory. It was second and seven on the twenty-eight and Mackin was searching out a receiver. *Crunch.* Down went Mackin for a loss of six. On the next play he tried a screen pass to his tight end. It worked. Almost. One yard short of the first down on the Cards' twenty-two. And time out Chargers.

Mackin trotted over to confer with Sims, hoping to convince

his coach to let him try for that yard. It was hardly typical Super Bowl play. Usually both teams spent the first half feeling each other out, going with draws, flares, rushes. And usually the hyped to hell Super Bowl turned out to be a big yawning bore. Nobody seemed to be yawning.

Apparently Mackin won his debate. He took the snap, a small step back. A hesitation. Then he snuck the ball right up the middle and vanished in a flurry of arms and legs. The crowd jumped to its feet, necks craned toward the day-glo yardsticks being trundled out onto the field. The official took one look and threw out his right arm. First down.

Then, quite simply, Mackin blew it again. On third down at the Cards' twelve, Mackin ducked the barreling safety and raced out of the pocket—right into the welcoming arms of the defensive end. Out came the field goal team to tie it up. But the snap was bad and the kick shot hopelessly off to the left. I glanced up at the clock and sighed.

A damp sheet of paper, smelling of mimeograph ink, floated down in front of me. First quarter statistics. I barely flicked them a glance because quarterback Max Wiggins was again coaxing the Cardinals downfield. They scored another field goal and Mackin continued brilliantly leading his team . . . nowhere.

The two-minute warning.

He would be mainly passing toward the sidelines now to stop the clock. It was like pulling teeth. A flare, an incompletion; a draw to the right side and the Chargers were on the Cardinals' thirty-seven with a minute five to go. Spencer Little, the other back, carried the ball to the thirty-two, and stepped out of bounds. Forty-five seconds. Mackin backpeddling, rearing to throw, a completion to his tight end. First down on the Cards' twenty-three.

Time out.

I lit another cigarette and tried not to notice how many butts were spilling out of my NFL ashtray. Thirty-eight seconds.

Mackin, taking the snap, moving back, his split end free down near the five. The pocket unraveling all over the place. Mackin throwing instead to his flanker, who was engaged in a foot race with the left linebacker. He had him beat, reached up for the ball.

And was hit by the strong safety.

Incomplete.

The clock stopped. Second down. Mackin moving back again. The blitz was on. He scrambled out of the pocket, found a hole, began running. At the last minute, he hurried a throw to Chip off to his right. Caught.

Flag down.

Illegal forward pass. Loss of 15. Third and 20 on the Cards' thirty-eight. Eleven seconds. Mackin had to get off a near perfect throw. He slipped back into the pocket, cocked his arm, threw a long pass toward his split end. Caught on the six-yard line—by the Cardinal's free safety.

The buzzer sounded.

I sat there frozen in my seat, my stomach all tied up in knots. I blocked out the commotion around me and thought. Okay, I told myself, he was moving the ball beautifully. Keeping the defense off balance, doing the unexpected, going for the weaknesses, gaining a lot of yardage. Until he got down to the nitty-gritty. Then he screwed up. The safety blitz. He had ducked the safety but then had run needlessly out of the pocket. He had seen a lineman coming at him so he had thrown into a crowd—like a goddamned rookie. He had a clear line to his split end and he threw to his flanker for an incompletion. He carried the ball past the line of scrimmage *then* threw a forward pass. You could blindfold a quarterback and he'd know where the line of scrimmage was. And now the interception, his *second*.

All those things and yet not one you could point to as deliberate. Little things, subtle things, things that could hap-

208

pen to any quarterback any day. Which, of course, was the whole point of a quarterback fix.

I climbed slowly out of my chair, walked down the corridor and hiked up to where all those fancy private boxes were located that the NFL had commandeered for the Super Bowl. All those people spending $20,000 to $50,000 a year for a box, had to find other seats for the Super Bowl. Because the NFL never awarded the big game to a stadium that denied them use of its private boxes. Still I didn't waste any sympathy on the private-box people.

I had arranged to meet my father in one of those boxes during half time. Ostensibly to check my information against his. But in fact, to get his opinion of Mackin's play.

I got it, loud enough for even Coach Sims to hear.

"Terrible! Terrible strategy," my father boomed. "Having Mackin throw like that in the first half. How does Sims expect him to keep going the rest of the game? Want a drink, honey?"

I said I'd better not.

"I think you ought to run down to the dressing room and talk to that quarterback of yours," he shouted. Several dozen glazed eyes rotated my way.

"What did you think of that last interception?" I asked.

"A real shame having him throw like that when he could have gone to Chip or Spencer. Do you realize he's already thrown twenty passes? It's insane."

"Jason Hollis! How the hell are you?"

Somebody in a pink jacket and long white sideburns lurched forward to shake Dad's hand and sloshed his drink on the carpeting. I kissed my father's cheek and slipped out into the corridor. Elbowed my way through an army of leisure suits and women with breasts hanging out of slinky dresses, amid the tinkle of ice cubes and high-pitched laughter.

As I walked back down the ramp, I wished vaguely that I had had a Scotch after all.

The Cardinals scored again.

Four minutes into the third quarter, Max Wiggins tossed a perfect 34-yard pass into the end zone.

Thirteen to nothing.

The Chargers got a break when the kick fell short and they ran the ball back to their own thirty-four. Fullback Spencer Little bulled for a six-yard gain; Chip picked up three more after that. Third and one. Mackin faked into the line, forcing the middle linebacker to freeze, then whipped off a pass to his tight end. Eleven yards. Down to the Cards' forty-six.

Mackin threw a bomb. It landed over the heads of every man on the field.

Mackin threw another bomb. The Card's free safety missed it by inches.

The next play he was sacked.

Finally, eight and a half minutes into the third quarter, Mike White managed a field goal to make it thirteen to three.

And that's the way the score stayed until three minutes into the fourth quarter. In two more calamitious series, the Cardinals had recovered a Charger fumble and Mackin had thrown . . . another interception.

The third quarter statistics appeared in front of me. The first half patterns were continuing to show up. Good solid play all down the field—then a subtle quarterback screw-up. If Dion had handed Mackin a game plan, it could not have been more perfect.

However.

A control pitcher could inexplicably walk the bases. An all-star shortstop could blow a crucial double play. And a quarterback who had been through the desert and hadn't worked out in two weeks . . .

Five minutes into the fourth quarter.

Once again the Chargers were chewing their way upfield. Across the fifty to the Cards' forty-four. And then, before I could wonder when he'd screw up again, Mackin was taking the snap. A long spiraling pass to his split end, Ralph Johnson. Johnson going back—catching it perfectly on the break, running now. Down to the Cardinals' eight. The pro-Mackin crowd sprang to life once again.

Eight measly yards.

I sank my teeth into a Super Bowl pen as Mackin set to pass. Nobody breaking clear. He hesitated but an instant then ran the ball himself right through the confused middle. *Thwack!* The collision carried clear up to the press box. One by one the bodies were removed until only Mackin lay on the ground. Flat on his stomach. With one scant inch of ball over the goal line. The head linesman threw up his arms to signal a touchdown and a zillion dots of color bobbed from Dome floor to Dome roof like a gargantuan kaleidoscope.

The specks of color separated and hung suspended.

Mackin did not get up.

The trainer hurried over to him. Mackin pointed emphatically to his right knee. Oh, God, I thought. Can't you think of anything original? And then, as if someone yanked the plug, the noise in the Superdome abruptly ceased.

Mackin struggled to his feet. Shook off the extended arms reaching out to him. Ha. I knew that old ploy. Athletes taking a long time to get up to win the sympathy of the crowd. Ploy or not, Mackin got it. He limped over to the sidelines amid thunderous applause and was immediately swallowed up by the

Chargers medical staff. Kick was good. Thirteen to ten. Five minutes to go.

I was crawling out of my skin. With one eye glued to the Chargers' bench and the other on the field, I semi-watched the Cardinals running for snatches of yardage to eat up the clock. Ball on their own thirty-two. To their thirty-eight. A short pass to the forty-five, another to the fifty, and it was beginning to look as if it wouldn't matter whether Mackin returned or not.

Wiggins was now almost forced to pass with the defense climbing all over fullback Hillary Smith, and Mike Jenkins, Scooter Sherwood's replacement, an uncertain ball carrier. Wiggins slipped back into the pocket. Ball up. Over the line of scrimmage. Arms outstretched. Deflection. And suddenly the Chargers' right linebacker was struggling to break loose with the ball. He was hit almost immediately. On his own thirty-seven.

Two minutes sixteen seconds. Out raced the Chargers' offense with Alexander Mackin in the lead; a slight limp as he hurried to the line. The crowd was screaming. A quick pass to his split end along the sidelines. Seven yards and the clock was stopped. Long huddle.

Thirteen to ten, I thought. Perfect. A spectacular touchdown and a faked knee injury. And it had all been so easy. He would probably emerge a hero anyway.

My eyes crawled across the painted signs hanging from the Dome railings. "Alex The Great! We Love You!" "Quintessential Quarterback, Quiet the Cards!" "Kidnap The Cards!" "Go Mighty Mack!"

I shivered and watched with tangled nerves as the Chargers crossed the fifty yard line. Two minute warning. And what if they had to go for the field goal? And White missed? Would anybody believe my allegations then?

The snap. Mackin passed. Incomplete. He gave the ball to

Little, who swept along the sidelines for six. A flare to the outside for five more and a first down. But dammit he *was* running a beautiful series. One minute twenty seconds. Another pass and the Chargers were on the twenty-eight. Second and three. Two plays later and they were on the twenty-two. Forty-six seconds. My stomach dropped to the floor.

An incompletion.

Mackin pitched out to Little who broke to his left for a four-yard gain before stepping out of bounds. They were down to the eighteen now on third and six. Absolute crucial play. Chip took the ball and plunged through the line. Out came the yardsticks. Dead silence. A foot short of the first down. They would have to kick after all. White would have to make a 29-yard field goal—against an eleven man rush.

From the Dome roof, a commercial tried to sell me life insurance. Too late, I thought. I had died five minutes ago. Poor Mike White was standing alone on the sidelines, shaking his arms, loosening his leg. And then he was walking lonesomely onto the field, and for one brief second, everything in the stadium froze. Not a movement, not a sound; even the clackety typewriters seemed to be holding their breath. The kick was up. Veering to the right. Still veering. And then before it could even register, the TV announcers were shrieking, "The kick is good! The kick is good! The Chargers have tied the game! It's sudden-death overtime, folks. What a game! Yessirree!"

My lungs collapsed. Now what? Come on, Quaid, now what do I do? What if he blows it in overtime? Doesn't matter. Doesn't count. Sorry, Quaid. The man down there wins, and to hell with you.

The Chargers lost the toss. Naturally the Cards elected to receive. Sudden death. Whoever scored first, won.

"Lindsie, could you please sit down, dear?" the reporter above me urged.

I didn't even know I was standing. I sat. The Cards ran the ball back to their own twenty-seven. I didn't care. Mackin was in the clear now, unless . . . Rushed for six yards. Wiggins passed for eight more. First down on their own forty-one. Wiggins lofted a bomb. Incomplete. Wiggins handed off to Mike Jenkins, Scooter's replacement. Jenkins tried a sweep to the left and was immediately hit by two clawing defensemen. The ball squirted out of his hands.

The Chargers recovered. On the Cards' forty-two.

I suddenly noticed the quiet man on my left staring at me. Had I been screaming? A field goal, I thought. Just one lousy field goal.

Mackin set the line and you could tell from the way he moved, how tired he was. He handed off to Chip who scratched out only three yards. Second down on the thirty-nine. Okay, Alex, just a little screen now. Mackin ignored me, faked to Spencer Little, then raced back and hoisted his arm. Chip was tearing downfield along the right sideline with a mere step on the linebacker, and in the split-second before the throw, I saw that play all over again flashing through my head. The same play which in that other Super Bowl had ended in an interception.

Chip was near the goal line and cutting to the inside. The ball and the free safety both on the way. Chip lunged and rolled into the end zone.

With the goddamn ball cradled in his arms.

The Friday after the Super Bowl game, I was home frantically pitching things into my suitcase for a week of skiing, when the doorbell rang. I pushed the intercom button and asked who it was.

"Mailman. Package for Miss Hollis."

Naturally I didn't push the buzzer. I walked down the four

flights of stairs to the foyer. In Boston, you don't trust even the mailman. And I wasn't expecting a package.

I crossed the lobby to the locked inner doors. I always peek through the glass windows first. I peeked and pushed open the door.

"Where's my package?" I demanded.

"I'm it."

"Alex, what are you doing here?"

He was clutching a suitcase in one hand and a copy of *Monday* magazine in the other. I looked from his grinning face on the cover to his grinning face on top of the brown suede jacket.

"Can I come in?"

"Are you selling magazines?"

"Goddammit, Lindsie."

We rode the elevator up to my apartment. I took his jacket and hung it in the closet, while he went over to inspect my bird.

"Jesus," he said. "You really do have a parakeet."

"Spot," I said, "this is Alex Mackin."

"Big deal," said my bird.

"Oh, Christ," said Mackin.

"Come sit," I invited.

We walked into the living room and sat. Mackin said, "I suppose you're wondering what I'm doing here?"

"Oh, no," I replied. "I'm just surprised you're here so soon. I only called the plant-sitter a little while ago."

Mackin grunted, fidgeted. "Did you hear they picked up Willy?" he said eventually.

I nodded. "In Tijuana. And I heard he has a nice long police record for armed assault."

"He's also wanted on suspicion of murder in New Mexico," said Mackin. "Jesus."

"And the plane," I went on. "They found Dion's plane and pilot all smashed up near the Arizona-Mexico border. Quaid thinks it was a bomb planted by Dion's imposter.''

Mackin studied his hands. "I wonder if they'll ever find him."

"They'll have to," I said, "if they want to prosecute Dion. Quaid said Willy insisted he thought the imposter was Dion, so he can't pin it on Dion either."

"No," said Mackin. "That's right."

He ran a knuckle across his mustache and stared at the coffee table. I sat there and stared at him.

"Would you like some coffee, or tea?"

"No thanks."

I smiled. "Okay, Alex, so why are you here?"

He cleared his throat. "Actually, I just wanted to thank you for the story. You're a good writer, Lindsie. And you were dead honest. I mean, you said some nice things and some not so nice things. I respect that." He shifted on the couch. "Though I'm not sure what you meant when you said that I treat my arm like a pedigreed Lhasa Apso."

"Why, thank you."

"Thank *you,*" he said, "for not printing this." He flipped open the magazine he had brought and handed me five type-written pages. My insert.

I stared at them. "Where did you get that?" I asked con-fusedly.

"Your boss gave it to me."

"Maxwell did?"

"Yeah. I went by the magazine first, and someone took me up to meet him. This would have killed me, Lindsie. The NFL could have suspended me permanently."

"I know."

"Then why? You could have printed it. Everything in there's the truth."

I shrugged and turned away from his direct gaze. "There just didn't seem any point, Alex. You did a dumb thing once and it didn't end up hurting anybody but you."

"No."

"So why print it? To prove to people that you're not perfect?" I started to reach for a cigarette then remembered there weren't any. I was trying to stop. "Anyway," I said, "I'm not so perfect either. I tried to be objective but . . ."

Mackin gave me a small smile. "I know. Nothing personal. But . . ." He hesitated. "Don't you think it's time we did get personal?"

"I'm flying to Denver . . ."

Mackin nodded solemnly. "In two hours. Then on to Keystone."

I looked at him. Slow lazy smile. Big green eyes. "Maxwell," I said with a sigh.

"Can't reveal my sources, ma'am. Anyway, I took the liberty of canceling your reservation."

"Alex . . ."

"And booking two first-class seats. I need the leg room."

Perhaps it was something that showed in my face. Or maybe, just because, he was so like me.

"After all," said Mackin, when I had hesitated too long, "it will be just for the week . . . a reunion." He smiled. "Old friends need reunions once in a while, don't you think?"